SO-ADS-423

"WE'RE GETTING MARRIED TODAY."

"It's the best plan. That way I can watch you around the clock and keep you safe while I find the stalker," Clay said.

Marisol slumped onto the bar stool, feeling as if the air had been knocked out of her lungs. "I'm *not* going to marry you, Clay!"

Despite her retort, Marisol was intrigued by Clay's marriage offer. She watched the corners of his mouth lift into a half smile and her attention focused on his eyes. They were dead serious. If he only knew how many times she had daydreamed about marriage.

"Do you always propose to the women you protect?" she asked.

"No. You're the first," he replied. Then in a husky voice Clay added, "Say yes, *Nena.*"

She was too honest to deny the strong physical attraction between them. She could feel the heat in Clay's dark, hooded gaze whenever he looked at her. He was so controlled and self-confident. His hot, hungry kisses from the previous evening had left her breathless, craving more. She wasn't sure how much longer they could remain platonic if they lived together.

<u>BOOK YOUR PLACE ON OUR WEBSITE</u>
<u>AND MAKE THE</u>
<u>READING CONNECTION!</u>

We've created a customized website just for our very special readers, where you can get the inside scoop on everything that's going on with Zebra, Pinnacle and Kensington books.

When you come online, you'll have the exciting opportunity to:

- View covers of upcoming books
- Read sample chapters
- Learn about our future publishing schedule (listed by publication month *and author*)
- Find out when your favorite authors will be visiting a city near you
- Search for and order backlist books from our online catalog
- Check out author bios and background information
- Send e-mail to your favorite authors
- Meet the Kensington staff online
- Join us in weekly chats with authors, readers and other guests
- Get writing guidelines
- AND MUCH MORE!

Visit our website at
http://www.pinnaclebooks.com

WILD FOR YOU

Victoria Marquez

PINNACLE BOOKS
KENSINGTON PUBLISHING CORP
http://www.encantoromance.com

PINNACLE BOOKS are published by

Kensington Publishing Corp.
850 Third Avenue
New York, NY 10022

Copyright © 2001 by Victoria Koch

All rights reserved. No part of this book may be reproduced in
any form or by any means without the prior written consent of
the Publisher, excepting brief quotes used in reviews.

If you purchased this book without a cover you should be
aware that this book is stolen property. It was reported as "un-
sold and destroyed" to the Publisher and neither the Author
nor the Publisher has received any payment for this "stripped
book."

All Kensington Titles, Imprints, and Distributed Lines are available at special quantity discounts for bulk purchases for sales
promotions, premiums, fund-raising, and educational or institu-
tional use. Special book excerpts or customized printings can
also be created to fit specific needs. For details, write or phone
the office of the Kensington special sales manager: Kensington
Publishing Corp., 850 Third Avenue, New York, NY 10022,
attn: Special Sales Department, Phone: 1-800-221-2647.

Pinnacle and the P logo, Encanto and the E logo Reg. U.S. Pat.
& TM Off.

First Printing: April 2001
10 9 8 7 6 5 4 3 2 1

Printed in the United States of America

With much love for my husband, Paul, and our two daughters, Genevieve and Jacqueline, who make life beautiful. For Pamela, Martha, and my sister Johanna, whose vocal enthusiasm delights me. And for my adorable niece, Natalie, who loves to write.

ACKNOWLEDGMENTS

Thank you to my mother, Emilia, for her generous spirit, to my dear Tia Julia who gave me wonderful books at an early age, and to my mother-in-law, Ines, whose deep inner strength inspires me.

In acknowledgment of my nephew, George, for his invaluable technical expertise. A big thank-you to my brother-in-law, Detective Jorge Mora, for answering all my questions with unflagging patience. In recognition of Sharon, Mariana, and Maria Eugenia, for their valued opinions, and Marisol and Nuri for their information. Also, special thanks to my editor, Tomasita Ortiz, and to my agent, Paige Wheeler, for making this dream come true.

One

"For Christ sake, Marcos, I'm a detective, not a baby-sitter," Clay muttered before taking a swig of cold beer.

"Marisol isn't a baby, as you'll soon find out." Dr. Marcos Calderon shifted on the bar stool. "I wouldn't be asking you to watch over her if I didn't think my little sister was in danger. Marisol owns the Villabella Beauty Salon in South Beach. She is so hell-bent on making it a success that she hasn't taken the anonymous messages as seriously as she should. I'm sure that she's not telling me the whole truth so that I won't get involved."

Clay's shoulders hunched forward as he leaned against the bar counter and studied his close friend. He understood Marcos's need to protect his little sister, especially since she had moved from Venezuela to live alone in a city like Miami. He took another sip of beer, then wiped the froth from his upper lip. "Why would she confide in me if she won't tell you?"

"It shouldn't be too hard to gain her confidence. Marisol is very outgoing and she has a tendency to be impulsive. Don't be fooled by her appearance, though. Marisol can be playful, but she's also very smart and used to getting her way. She's damned stubborn, too." He shook his head. *"Caramba,* if I'd been able to get her to stay in Naples where I could keep an eye on her, she wouldn't be in this predicament."

Clay met Marcos's gaze squarely. "Is there anything else you'd like to warn me about your little sister?"

"Yeah. When it comes to men, Marisol is a magnet."

Clay snorted and leaned back on the bar stool.

Marcos chuckled dryly. "You'll have to attract her attention, then gain her trust so you can find out exactly what's going on. I have to get back to my patients tomorrow morning. Will you do it, Che?"

Marcos had begun calling Clay "Che" a long time ago when he had learned Clay was part Argentinian on his mother's side. Wanting to help his friend, Clay smiled at him. "Of course I'll look into it. You've never asked me for a favor, even though I sure owe you one."

"You don't owe me anything." Marcos gave him an affectionate clap on the back. "I know she'll be in good hands now . . . thanks for agreeing. You can start by visiting her salon for a haircut," he said, eyeing Clay's ponytail.

"Yeah, well, now that I'm working homicide, I don't need long hair anymore for undercover work. I've never set foot inside a prissy beauty salon, but I'll do it for you." Clay looked up at the ceiling and sighed with resignation. "Where does Marisol live?"

"She has a condominium at Porto Sereno."

Marisol Calderon studied the lean planes of her client's face. He sat before her waiting for a haircut, his brown, corded arms braced on the leather armchair. He wore snug, faded Levi's with a plain black T-shirt tucked in, his pitch-black, shoulder-length hair in a ponytail. A small scar marked his left cheekbone on deeply tanned, olive skin. A tiny shiver unexpectedly tingled her spine when she glanced at his intense black eyes, deep set and heavily rimmed by long black lashes.

The man looked so out of place in her salon that she wondered if he could be the anonymous stranger who had been pestering her lately with phone calls. She applied conditioner to his scalp, determined to detain him long enough to find out.

He jerked up and glanced over his shoulder. "What are you doing?" When he spoke, his chiseled lips parted to reveal strong white teeth.

"Relax, it's an all-natural conditioner. Your hair looked a little dry."

"I asked for a haircut, not a beauty treatment."

She patted his shoulder. "Don't worry, it's my special this week. The conditioner is included in the price of the haircut. It won't cost you a penny extra."

"I'm not worried about the cost. What's in this *all-natural* conditioner? It stinks."

"Mashed avocado and olive oil," she replied matter-of-factly. "Did you say your name was Clay?"

"Yeah."

"Marisol!" the receptionist at the front desk called out. "Phone call."

Marisol gave Clay an apologetic smile. "I'm needed at the front desk. I'll put you under the dryer first to speed up the conditioning."

"Forget it. Hurry back or I'll wash it out myself," he warned. Clay shifted his body in the pink leather chair and reminded himself that he was doing this as a favor for Marcos.

Marisol tossed her head, shaking her blond-streaked, honey-brown hair, and shrugged her delicate shoulders. Clay distinctly heard her mutter *"Que impaciente"* in a Venezuelan accent as she brushed by him, pert backside swaying. He couldn't believe that she had just called him impatient, when she was the source of his discomfort.

He felt like snarling. The mashed avocado mixture was beginning to seep into his scalp. Glancing across the gleaming, art-deco style pink and black salon, he watched Marisol chatting animatedly.

There was nothing demure about Marisol Calderon. She wore dangling hoop earrings and a knit tangerine minidress that hugged her petite, curvaceous frame. On her feet were matching high-heeled sandals. Clay watched Marisol laugh delightedly on the telephone and tap her long, lacquered nails against the reception counter.

This little piece of fluff was going to be a handful.

Clay was beginning to see that Marisol wasn't the ditzy Latina she had initially appeared to be. Her fresh, olive-toned complexion and short, tousled hair made her look younger than twenty-nine. Earlier, he had noticed the radiant wit in her hazel cat eyes and the tiny, impudent cleft gracing her chin. Her full-lipped mouth naturally curved upward at the corners, giving her a decidedly mischievous air.

He wasn't keen about having to deceive her, but there was no other way. Her brother had insisted that Marisol not be told of Clay's connection with Marcos so that she would not refuse his help. Marisol hated being looked after by her big brother so much that she had left Naples as soon as she had inherited the trust fund from her grandfather.

When the first drop of avocado mixture began sliding down his neck, he squared his shoulders and rose from the chair, carefully avoiding the potted philoden-dron to his right. With purposeful strides, he headed toward the reception desk. At that moment Marisol turned to face him and wisely terminated the tele-phone conversation.

Eyeing Clay with an impish grin, she said, "Sorry that took so long." She glanced at her watch. "You still have five minutes left on the conditioner." Grab-bing a flowered plastic cap in her hands, she walked toward him. "Since you refuse to go under the dryer, let's put this cap over your hair to speed things up."

He leveled a stern look at her. "No way. Get this stuff out of my hair. I feel like a walking salad."

"You have a great voice," she observed, unable to contain her widening grin. "Sounds like gravel rub-bing against marble."

Clay let out a strangled groan.

"But you sound a little tense," she added quickly. Maybe if she offered to massage his shoulders, she could disarm him enough so that he would talk more about himself. "This beauty treatment includes a little massage during the last five minutes of the conditioner."

With obvious reluctance, he lowered himself into the chair in front of the shampoo sink. Marisol placed both hands on either side of his neck and firmly rotated the tips of her thumbs against his nape. "Your neck feels all bunched up in knots. Just relax," she coaxed. "How did you find my salon? Did somebody recommend me?"

Clay shook his head. "I picked up one of your fly-ers at the building where I live. You claimed to use only organic products and I was curious."

"Where do you live?"

"A development called Porto Sereno."

"Oh," Marisol replied, surprised that he lived in the

same building she did. How had she missed someone
as compelling as him? When he first entered her
salon, she'd noticed his wary stance and watchful
eyes. He had asked for a haircut in a smoky voice that
instantly grabbed her attention. Instead of giving him
to one of her stylists, Marisol had been intrigued
enough to attend to him herself.

She refrained from telling him that she also lived at
Porto Sereno. For all she knew, this man could be the
one leaving those anonymous messages. She would
have to casually draw him into conversation in order to
find out. Caution was not usually one of Marisol's qualities, but since the suspicious phone calls had begun,
she was trying to temper her openness with restraint.

Marisol opted to discuss her favorite subject.
"Many of my treatments originated in the finest salons
in Venezuela. You know how Venezuela is famous for
its beauty pageant queens."

Clay nodded, but from the way his shoulders stiff-
ened beneath her hands she could tell he wasn't interested in beauty talk. He was so different from the
models and actors who frequented her salon that she
wondered again why he had chosen to come to her es-
tablishment for a haircut.

"Since we use natural products made from fruits and
vegetables, our customers always return for more. You'll
see how shiny your hair looks after just one treatment!"

"I can hardly wait."

Ignoring his dry tone, Marisol continued the massage. "You have a great tan. Do you work outdoors?"

"Sometimes." He paused. "I'm the new security
manager at Porto Sereno."

Intrigued, she remembered that the previous security manager had just been transferred to Fisher Is-

land. Her client would have to possess excellent credentials to be hired as a security manager in her exclusive complex. "Have you worked there long?" she asked. If he said yes, she would know he was an impostor.

"No. I was hired this month."

"The social director there is a friend of mine." Marisol lied. "Maybe you know her. Sylvia Rodriguez?"

Clay's brow furrowed. "No. Bill Gomez is the social director. From what he told me, he's been there since it was built."

"Really? Then Sylvia must work for him," Marisol said, satisfied by his answer. "Do you like working there?"

His broad shoulders shrugged. "Yeah. But I won't be there for long."

"Why not?"

"I'm a law student. I'll be taking the bar exam soon."

He certainly didn't look like a college student! More like a renegade. "A law student?" she asked, thinking that he had to be in his midthirties.

He nodded and glanced at his watch. "Isn't it time to wash out this goop?"

"Yes. Lean your head back and I'll shampoo it, then I'll style your hair."

She lathered the shampoo in with the fleshy pads of her fingertips, stroking his scalp and hair in circulating movements as she worked out the last of the conditioner.

"That feels great."

"Thanks." Marisol turned off the water and wrapped Clay's hair turban style in a white cotton towel, which he promptly pulled off. *"Venga,"* she said, motioning for him to follow her as she walked toward an empty chair. "You can sit there."

Clay complied, lowering himself into the chair.

"Would you like *una colada* or *café con leche?*" Marisol asked. "We have a new machine and Rosa's an expert at it."

"No coffee, thanks. Just a haircut."

Marisol stood behind him and scrutinized his features in the mirror before them. "We'll keep your sideburns the same length, but since your hair is straight and coarse, I'd like to trim it much shorter," she said, combing his hair. "Unless you want to keep it long enough for a ponytail."

"No. The ponytail can go."

Clay sat rigidly while Marisol divided his hair into sections. She followed his gaze to the door as a plain white delivery truck arrived. The delivery man handed the receptionist a large bouquet of orchids and birds of paradise.

"Marisol!" the receptionist called again. "There's a delivery for you."

Marisol left Clay sitting with his wet hair divided into sections held by large metal clips. Her provocative strut commanded his attention as his gaze followed the sultry sway of her shapely hips. That was one thing she'd have to modify if he was to safeguard her. With a walk like that, she surely drew too much attention for her own good.

Clay tried to collect his wits. Marisol had proved to be sneakily persuasive. With an alluring smile, she had managed to coax him into a neck and shoulder massage after she had applied the mashed avocado to his hair without his consent. He made a mental note to sharpen his defenses against her charm.

He watched Marisol's face as she read the card attached to the floral arrangement. Her curious expression quickly turned to anger. She glanced up, and as her eyes met Clay's from across the room, he noted how she tried to appear calm.

When she returned to him with the card still in her hand, Clay casually asked, "Is today your birthday?"

"No." Marisol pulled open the drawer in front of him and placed the card inside, facedown.

"Then the flowers are from your boyfriend?"

Marisol's eyes, so lively when he had first met her, now held a shadow of apprehension. "I don't have a boyfriend. They're from a friend."

"Marisol," called the young woman at the front desk yet again. "There's a call for you."

"Luz, just take a message," Marisol said, exasperated.

"But it's the landlord. He says it's urgent!" Luz whined.

Sighing out loud, Marisol said, "Okay, tell him to hold on." Turning to Clay, she said, "I'm really sorry about all the interruptions. Things are usually not this hectic, but the new receptionist seems to think that every phone call is urgent."

Clay leaned back in the chair. "Don't worry. Take your time."

With an apologetic smile, she hurried to the reception area and picked up the telephone.

While her back was turned, Clay reached inside the drawer and retrieved the florist's card. He read it silently:

Marry me. I'm so hot for you it hurts.

The message was typed on a plain white card without the name of the florist shop. He replaced the card in the drawer before Marisol could catch him reading it.

When Marisol returned, she looked upset. "What's wrong?" Clay asked.

"It wasn't my landlord—it was the guy who sent the bouquet. I wonder how he knew the flowers had arrived." She bit her lower lip. "I can't seem to get rid of him. He's becoming a terrible nuisance."

"Have you contacted the police?"

"No, but I will now." She grimaced with distaste, then straightened her spine. "Can we change the subject?"

"Sure." Clay gave her a disarming grin that transformed his austere face. "How about dinner tonight?"

Entranced, Marisol stared at the dimples framing his sexy half smile. She blinked to tear herself from his dark eyes, which appeared warm and sincere. She wanted to agree instantly, but she didn't.

"I never mix business with pleasure," she said. Clay's look of genuine disappointment pleased her, since she sensed that his impromptu invitation had been out of character for someone so composed. She stared at his left hand and noted there was no wedding band. "How do I know you're not married?"

He gave her a sharp look. "I wouldn't ask you out if I was."

"Oh," she said, liking his answer and wondering why she felt compelled to believe him. Everything about Clay intrigued her, and she wanted to know more. Impulsively, she said, "If you tell me about yourself, I might agree to have dinner with you."

"My name is Clay Blackthorne. What else do you want to know?"

"Where are you from? You look Latino, but your last name isn't."

"My mother's Argentinian. I was named after my father who was American."

No wonder his thick, glossy hair was so black that it looked blue. Tilting her head, she examined his features. "With your sharp cheekbones and hawk nose, you definitely look Argentinian. Do you speak Spanish?"

"*Sí.*"

"Were you raised in Miami?" Marisol asked, lifting strands of his hair and clipping them.

"No. What about you?"

"I was born in Venezuela, but I went to college in Miami, then moved to Naples with my brother. Last year I moved back to Miami. Even though I miss my family, I love it here!" She studied him. "Are you *really* a law student?"

"I already graduated. I'm taking the bar exam this fall."

"Great! Maybe you can give me some advice on how to handle my greedy landlord."

A slight smile tugged at his lips. "We can discuss it over dinner tonight."

Despite his enigmatic appearance, Clay's candid answers made her want to trust him. Marisol blow-dried his freshly cut hair without responding to his invitation. Lifting several strands of his hair at a time, she brushed the sides back to blend in with the hair over his neck, which she'd left slightly longer. When it was dry, she dipped a large sable brush in talcum powder and swept it across the back of his neck. Handing him a round mirror so he could see the back of his hair, she asked, "How do you like it?"

He glanced in the mirror. "Looks fine. What time do you close shop?"

Marisol hesitated before answering. "Seven o'clock on weeknights."

"Great." Clay's dark gaze held hers. "Do you like Thai food?"

She was drawn to his fathomless black eyes. "Yes, sometimes, but . . ."

"There's a great Thai restaurant in the Grove. How about if I pick you up here at seven?" Standing now, he handed her the plastic cape that had been covering his broad shoulders, then strode toward the receptionist.

"Wait a minute," Marisol protested, hastening to match his long strides. "I didn't say I'd go out with you."

He turned to face her and there was that slow smile again, deeply dimpled and very persuasive. "Wasn't it your idea to ask a few questions before agreeing to have dinner with me?"

"You're twisting my words," she protested lamely, still riveted by his penetrating gaze. Marisol didn't really need to think twice about it; she knew she would have dinner with him. She couldn't allow whoever was sending her flowers to make her become paranoid of everyone. That just wasn't in her nature.

Clay was more self-possessed than any man she had ever met. She liked that he had been a good sport and tolerated the avocado conditioner despite obvious discomfort. It hadn't been very professional of her, but it was the only way she could think of to keep him there long enough to find out if he was the one harassing her. Besides, her practical side reminded her that she could ask Clay for legal advice concerning her business lease.

"All right, I'll have dinner with you," she said. "But we go in separate cars."

"Fine," he agreed immediately.

"Until seven, then." Marisol nodded at him, then

turned and walked toward the reception desk to greet her next client.

Clay paid the receptionist before stepping out into the blistering July afternoon. He pulled on his tinted sunglasses to shade his eyes from the harsh sunlight. Thoughts of Marisol and her situation invaded his mind when he got into his black 1980 Firebird. He was amazed that despite the predicament she was in, Marisol's personality remained basically upbeat. He had never met anyone so exuberant.

His sunglasses suddenly fogged up from the steamy interior. It had been heating up with Miami's hot sun. He smiled wryly, wondering if the real reason for misty sunglasses was his recent session with Marisol. During the shampoo, Marisol's shapely bosom had been close as she bent over him to rinse out the conditioner. With her curves hovering inches above his face, his body had responded instantly and he'd had to close his eyes. But her nearness had been so tantalizing that he'd had a hard time ignoring her, even with his eyes shut.

She had bombarded his senses quickly and thoroughly. He was staggered by how strong a physical effect she'd had on him in such a short time. He shook his head to dispel the distraction and the pang of guilt he felt when he thought of how Marcos would feel about his attraction to his kid sister.

He glanced at his watch. Four hours left before he was to meet her at the salon. He wanted to touch base with Marcos and report his progress.

Clay was disturbed that Marisol had accepted a date so readily, without knowing who he was. Sure, she had asked a few questions initially, but for someone who had just received flowers and a note with strong sexual innuendos, she wasn't being cautious enough about her personal life.

Marcos wouldn't be happy to hear about it. Six years her senior, he had been fiercely protective of Marisol ever since she had moved away from her family in Venezuela to start an independent life in the States.

When Clay finished work, he returned to Marisol's salon. As he approached the building he almost mistook the receptionist Luz, as she locked the front door of the salon, for Marisol. There was a striking similarity in their hairstyles and coloring, but the resemblance ended there. When he reached her side, Clay noted that the receptionist had a fuller figure than Marisol, and seemed taller.

"Where's Marisol?" Clay asked.

Luz whirled around. *"Ay,* you startled me! I didn't hear you walk up!" she exclaimed, clasping a hand to her chest. She stared at Clay's feet. "Where did you learn to walk so silently? You shouldn't sneak up on people like that."

"I wasn't sneaking up on you. Marisol and I made plans for dinner tonight. Is she still inside?"

Luz shifted her feet uneasily. "She left about fifteen minutes ago with a terrible migraine. She had to make a bank deposit first, and then she wanted to go home to lie down. She said she'd take a rain check on dinner with you."

Irritation sliced through Clay's composure. He hated unpredictability, especially today. Forcing a smile, he said, "All right, I'll come by tomorrow. Thanks for the message."

Clay got into his car and drove directly to Marisol's

apartment. If he hurried, he might intercept her at the door and get some answers. He didn't believe the story about her headache. She'd been too lively that afternoon to suddenly have such a headache so debilitating that she had to go home and lie down. Why had she stood him up? The thought of foul play nagged at him.

He stood outside her door and jabbed her doorbell several times. No answer. He folded his arms and leaned his shoulder against the door frame, determined to wait it out. Fifteen minutes later he heard the elevator doors open and shut; then high heels tapped on the tile floor, signaling Marisol's arrival.

When Marisol saw Clay, she stepped backward awkwardly and lost her balance. Her take-out dinner flew across the hall like a frisbee. She landed smack on her behind, on the dry cleaning she'd just picked up.

Her heartbeat accelerated as she peered up at Clay, hoping that he hadn't noticed how her short skirt had hiked up to indecent levels. She grasped the hem with both hands and yanked it down over her thighs. "What are you doing here?"

Clay reached out to help her up. "I work here, remember? Your receptionist told me you left with a bad migraine. I came by to see how you were feeling."

Goose bumps prickled her arm when Clay's warm, steady hand helped her to her feet. "Luz told you where I live?"

"She didn't have to. I know all the tenants' names." Still holding her arm, he gently pulled her a little closer. "Why did you stand me up tonight?"

His appealing scent, a heady mixture of evergreen and maleness, sent tiny shivers racing through her body. She glanced at Clay's chiseled lips hovering inches from her face, and his low voice assailed her senses. She stepped back and he released her arm. Marisol winced as she put pressure on her left foot. She knew it was hurt. "Luz told you—I have a horrible headache."

His night-black eyes challenged her. "Funny. You don't look sick to me." Clay leaned against her door frame again and crossed his arms, deep brown and corded with lean muscle. "You're not a very convincing liar."

"All right." Marisol sighed out loud. "Shortly after you left, that weirdo called me again. I called the police, but nobody there took me seriously. The detective I spoke with said that the anonymous caller hasn't done anything illegal until he threatens bodily harm."

Clay's mouth tightened. "Unfortunately, it's true. Even though stalking is considered a felony in Florida, sending flowers and notes doesn't constitute a crime unless there's proof that the person is out to physically harm you."

"You sound just like the detective I talked to," she muttered. "Anyway, after that depressing bit of info, I regretted accepting your dinner invitation so impulsively. I told Luz to excuse me so I could ask the security guard downstairs about you."

"How did I check out?" Clay asked confidently.

"With flying colors. *Caramba!* Once Alan started raving about your qualifications, I couldn't shut him up."

"Alan's a good man." He paused for a moment. "Do you recognize the voice of the person who called you at the salon?"

"No. His voice is always muffled. For the past few weeks, he's called my home number and left messages on my recording machine. I changed my number, but he got my new, unlisted one. Today was the first time he called me at work, twice." A shiver wracked her body. "His voice gives me the creeps. It's sort of high-pitched and nasal."

"What did he say?"

"That I belong to him and he won't stop until we're married."

"Did you reply?"

"No! I hung up on him."

Clay nodded. "Good. Let me help you inside. Better not put any pressure on your foot till I can check it. Lean against me."

"I can manage walking by myself." Marisol fumbled inside her handbag. "Where are my keys? I really need to clean out this purse." After a few moments spent searching for her keys, she smiled triumphantly. "Here they are!" When she attempted to lean down and pick up her dry cleaning, her left leg almost buckled beneath her. "I'd better get off these heels."

Clay picked up her dry cleaning from the floor. Marisol stretched out her hand. "I'll take that," she said, wanting him to leave before she unlocked the door.

"Listen, you can't even stand without hurting your foot. And your dinner is ruined. Let me order pizza for us." He walked over and picked up the remnants of her scattered take-out.

Marisol's growling stomach conquered her doubt. "Okay. I guess you can come in, but only because you're *el jefe* of security around here. I suppose you should be aware of what's been going on." She braced her weight on her uninjured foot and opened her front door. "Come in."

Clay draped the dry cleaning over one arm, then effortlessly lifted Marisol's petite form in his arms and carried her into the apartment. Closing the door with his foot, he glanced around as he entered. Her apartment was as vibrant as her personality. Marisol had decorated with bright colors and an eclectic mix of furniture. On the lemon yellow walls, watercolor paintings of wild birds and tropical landscapes intensified the vividness of the decor.

Clay looked down at Marisol's flushed face, inches away from his. Her coral pink mouth, busily protesting being carried, was tempting him with its velvety fullness. Forcing his eyes away, he strode to the center of her living room and placed her on a large, overstuffed sectional. Across the room, the dining room table had a verdigris iron base topped with a round glass top. In the center, a ceramic vase brimmed with yellow and white daisies.

Marisol kicked off her sandals and wiggled her toes. "Ah, what a relief!"

Clay sat in an armchair and stretched his legs in front of him, crossing one ankle over his knee. He observed Marisol, who resembled a bewitching Persian kitten as she curled up in the center of the sectional. Noting Marisol's weakening effect on his concentration, he sat up straight.

"Would you like a glass of chardonnay?" she asked. "I don't have any beer."

"Chardonnay is fine," he answered. "Stay there. I'll get it when I order the pizza. What do you want on it?"

"Everything, including anchovies. That is, if you like them, too."

"I do." Clay went into the kitchen to order the pizza and sat next to her on the sectional when he returned. "How's your foot?"

Marisol stood to test it. "Much better, not even a twinge." She walked to the kitchen and spoke to him through the pass-thru window. "You forgot the wine," she said, then smiled at his apologetic shrug.

When she returned to the living room with the two glasses of wine, Clay's surprised glance traveled the length of her petite body.

"Why are you looking at me that way?" she asked, handing him a wineglass.

"I was just thinking how small you are without your high heels."

"Oh, that." She wrinkled her nose and waved her hand in dismissal. "I hate being short, so I wear the highest heels I can tolerate."

Clay gave her a perplexed look. "I don't see why you bother."

"You would if you were just five feet tall, instead of six feet," she replied with a toss of her head. "On high heels, I don't feel at such a disadvantage next to those towering fashion models who come into my salon."

He smiled. "I see your point." But his expression suddenly grew somber. "Your answering machine light was blinking in the kitchen."

"I noticed. I'll check it later. I don't feel like dealing with another weird message."

Clay leveled a direct look at her. "Don't you have any idea who it might be?"

She shrugged, then took a sip of the chilled wine. "Not a clue. I meet so many people at my shop, and also at the gym where I work out. I can't narrow it down to any man in particular." For a long moment, she regarded him with curiosity. "You seem very interested in whoever is harassing me."

"It's my job."

Marisol tilted her head sideways, her lips quirking up at the corners. "Is that all?"

"What do you think?"

She raised her brows slightly, and shrugged her shoulders. Strolling into the kitchen and opening the cabinet, she neatly avoided his question. "I think it's time to get the table ready. The pizza should be here soon."

He followed her into the kitchen. "Need any help?"

"You can set the table while I make a salad." Marisol switched on the compact disc player and inserted a CD. "Shakira always gives me a boost of energy."

Clay would have preferred new age guitar or classical, but he amused himself by watching Marisol as she sang a little off-key and moved to the music with uninhibited ease. She took out peach linen place mats, matching napkins, aqua plates, and cutlery. After preparing a salad of mixed baby greens, Marisol blended a balsamic vinaigrette for the salad.

"Looks good. Do you like to cook?" he asked.

"Sometimes, if I get inspired. I really miss Abuelita Coqui's cooking." She sighed. "Especially the *hallacas* she makes at Christmastime."

"What are *hallacas?*" Clay asked, noting the wistful smile on her face.

"They're like the Cuban *tamale*, only larger, square-shaped and wrapped in plantain leaves. In Venezuela, they stuff them with a filling of corn meal, potato, and tasty meats." She tossed the salad and tasted a dark green lettuce leaf. "Can you cook?"

"Yeah, I enjoy it," he said.

Marisol stared at him. "Really? Somehow I can't imagine you as a gourmet cook."

Clay laughed. "No, nothing like that. I make stir-fry."

"Aren't you part Argentinian? I would have figured you for a *parillada* man."

"Oh, sure. I make a mean *parillada*, too. There's no science to making a good barbecue."

The doorbell rang just as she placed the salad bowl in the center of the table. Clay answered the door and shoved a few extra dollars into the delivery man's hand. He returned to the table bearing the large carton.

Marisol served him a slice and helped herself to one, too. As she took a small bite and began to chew, his gaze was instantly drawn to her lush mouth. He watched her small pink tongue dart out to lick a spot of tomato sauce lingering on her full lower lip. He found himself wondering how Marisol would taste, how her lips would look, rosy and swollen from his kisses. He reacted strongly to the thought, his body filled with desire. Sternly reminding himself that she was Marcos's kid sister and therefore off-limits, he reached for another slice and looked away from her tantalizing mouth.

"Where do you live?" Marisol asked.

"In this building. The apartment is one of the perks of my job. The best part is the view," he said, gesturing toward the sliding-glass doors that led to the balcony. Below was a pristine lake surrounded by massive banyan trees and lofty royal palms.

"My brother Marcos and I own this apartment and another one in this building."

"What made you move to Miami?"

She grimaced. "I needed a little breathing space. As the only daughter, my parents and extended family in Venezuela have always clucked over me like mother hens. They've been involved in everything I do, from urging me to get a business degree, to nagging me to settle down, get married, and have kids." She smiled.

"Even though I love children, they're not in my immediate plans."

"What are your immediate plans?"

"To show my family that *la niña,* as they refer to me," she said, rolling her eyes, "can succeed at building a spectacular beauty business. Poor Marcos. During his residency, he was appointed by the family to keep an eye on me while I attended the University of Miami. He used to complain about my constant partying at night when I was really attending beauty school."

"Why didn't you just tell him the truth?"

"Because he would have opposed my goal to open a beauty salon. After I graduated with my business degree and got my beautician's license on the side, I had already received part of Abuelito's trust fund and I was ready to start my business. But first, I went back to Venezuela to get some experience."

"In what?"

"The beauty business, of course. I was lucky to get an apprenticeship working with top models and beauty contestants," she said. "That's where I met Gustavo."

"Who's Gustavo?"

"The man I loved, or at least thought I did. When I sent word to Marcos that we were engaged, he went ballistic and had Gustavo investigated. I think Abuelita was in on everything, too, since her goal in life is to marry me off to the right man. But I didn't believe the negative report that Marcos's investigator produced, so I kept dating Gustavo until I realized Marcos had been right about him. Gustavo was a bit of a con man."

That was putting it mildly, Clay thought to himself. From what Marcos had confided in him about Gustavo, the guy was a real snake and Marisol was fortunate to be rid of him. "That still doesn't explain why you moved down here," Clay reminded her, wondering why most women had to tell a story just to answer a simple question.

"When I joined Marcos in Naples, it was obvious I'd have to move away. I desperately needed to be on my own and Marcos was taking his role as my guardian too seriously. Even though he's a busy surgeon, his need to keep me on what he considered the right path was stifling." She shook her head. "I love him, but he distrusts most men, and thinks they're all players like him."

Clay chuckled. What Marisol had just said about Marcos was right on target. Marcos was such a successful obstetrician that he had often joked that he didn't have time to make a serious commitment. Clay believed that his buddy was having too much fun casually dating to want to curb his freedom.

"Don't laugh! Venezuelan men can be very possessive of the women in their lives, especially little sisters. I wish he could find a woman to monopolize his attention, so he could give me a break!"

The ringing telephone interrupted their conversation. Marisol stared at the telephone with apprehension before picking it up. She listened for a few moments, then slammed down the receiver and dashed to the door. Clay was beside her in an instant.

"What is it?" he demanded.

She opened the door and pointed to a small, wrapped parcel lying on the floor. "Look!"

He bolted down the hall toward the elevator, scanning both sides of the hallway, then returned, disgusted that he hadn't found anyone. "Whoever dropped this off is long gone. Next time let me check the door first." Picking up the package, he carried it to the table with Marisol in tow. "I'll call downstairs and alert Alan to check for an intruder. In the meantime, open the package."

Immobilized, Marisol stood beside Clay as he made the call. When he hung up, she blurted out, "I can't bring myself to open it."

Clay handed her the package. "Aren't you curious about what's inside?"

She swallowed, her eyes clouded with anguish. "If I open it now, it'll only ruin our evening."

"Then I'll open it for you," Clay said firmly.

Marisol frowned. "Oh, never mind, I can manage." She tore open the package and lifted the cover off the box, gasping when she parted the black tissue paper and saw what was inside.

Red satin-covered handcuffs.

She picked them up for closer inspection, then returned her attention to the card inside the box. Her body froze and she seemed unable to bring herself to read the message.

"Let me see the card," Clay said, taking over.

Marisol took a deep, shuddering breath. "No. I'll read it." In a tremulous voice, she read the sloppy print aloud: "I'm going to bind you to me and relish watching you struggle. Tonight."

She dropped the note as if it were in flames.

Wanda Morgan

Two

"Where are the other notes he sent?" Clay demanded.

Marisol took a large sip of wine to calm herself. "I threw them out."

"Did they have any kinky messages or sexual overtones like this one?"

Marisol shook her head. "No. That's what baffles me. It's almost as if this guy has a split personality."

"Why do you say that?"

"Because at first he was just friendly and seemed to be flirting with me. But the messages are getting nastier. His voice doesn't sound the same each time he calls either, even though most of the time he mentions marrying me. This last call was mostly animal grunts and heavy breathing." Marisol shuddered as she shredded her napkin into rows. "Today was the first time I ever received anything besides flowers."

"Don't you have *any* clue of who it could be?" he asked. "An ex-boyfriend maybe?"

"No. Even though I was the one to break it off, Gustavo's not the type to hide behind notes and gifts. He's too conceited for that."

"Have you had any other boyfriends since then?"

She paused to study him before replying, "Do I have to answer that?"

"I'm trying to help you solve this."

"I don't mind your questions. Truth is, after Gustavo, nobody has interested me beyond casual dating."

Clay hoped his impassive expression hid the satisfaction he felt at her candid admission. Even though she was unpredictable and too impulsive for her own good, Marisol affected him like a ray of sunshine, vital, warm, and invigorating.

Taking a slow sip of wine, he asked, "Have you told your brother about this?"

She shook her head emphatically. "If I told Marcos that the police had dismissed my complaints, he'd be here in a flash. He's been hounding me to hire a private eye ever since I mentioned that somebody had been sending me flowers with strange anonymous messages."

Clay drummed his fingers on the table. "You should listen to good common sense."

Her expression turned belligerent. "I do not want Marcos interfering in my life!"

"I'd be worried if it were happening to my little sister." Clay silently amended, *Thank God you're not my sister.*

Marisol sighed. "I know. But after the fiasco with Gustavo, I need to convince Marcos and the rest of my family that I'm capable of handling things without their interference. It's depressing that at twenty-nine, I still have to prove myself," she said, her large hazel eyes wounded. "Tomorrow, I'll start looking for a private detective. I just hope that whoever's tormenting me will grow bored and find some other way to get his kicks. I can't be the only woman he's interested in."

"Sometimes a stalker becomes so obsessed with his victim, he'll do anything to be with her." Clay's

unswerving gaze penetrated hers as he repeated,
"Anything."

Marisol straightened her spine. "If I show him I'm
a scared, weak opponent, he'll use that to his advantage. Do you know anyone I can hire to investigate
this?"

"You're looking at him. Play the messages on your
recording machine before I leave tonight. There might
be a similar message." The brackets beside his hard
mouth deepened as he smiled briefly, but Marisol noticed the smile didn't quite reach his eyes. "I studied
criminal law. I can help you solve this puzzle."

Despite the grave circumstances, Marisol was
drawn to those sexy dimples. "Cute dimples. Too bad
you don't smile more often."

Clay's smile flattened into a firm, implacable line.
"Don't change the subject. Let's hear those messages."

"You and Marcos should meet sometime and discuss a few negative traits you have in common, like
bossiness." With a toss of her head, Marisol marched
to the kitchen and punched the message button on her
machine.

Soft music preceded a muffled message. "Baby, did
you like my flowers? When you open my gift, change
into something tight and black. We'll practice for our
honeymoon. I can't wait to make you squirm."

Marisol's stomach lurched. The threats were no
longer veiled and cryptic—this one was clearly twisted.

"I want a copy of the tape," Clay said, dialing in the
numbers to call Alan again. When he finished ques-
tioning him, he hung up and turned to Marisol. "Alan
just told me he hasn't admitted any visitors into the
building this evening since his shift started. And he
didn't notice anyone strange leaving the building

since I called him earlier. The stalker might live in this same building. Did you ever consider that?"

Marisol shuddered, despite her effort to control the rising panic inside of her. "Yes. The thought has crossed my mind," she admitted, her heart thumping.

Clay leveled a determined look at Marisol. "I'd like to stay and protect you tonight until you can get a private investigator working on this tomorrow."

Marisol gawked at him. "Do you honestly believe that I'd allow you to spend the night in my apartment?"

"Sure," he replied as if he did that sort of thing all the time.

"You're crazy. You know that?"

"Sunshine, you're the crazy one if you think I'm leaving you at the mercy of some pervert tonight. You can lock your bedroom door while I sleep on the sofa."

"You're taking your new security responsibilities too far. Besides, I haven't hired you as a bodyguard. I wouldn't consider letting a stranger sleep in my living room, unless it was a matter of life and death."

"I'm not a stranger," he protested. "We've shared pizza and our pasts with each other. What more do you want?"

"I'm the one who's been doing most of the talking," she reminded him.

"This could be a matter of life and death. You don't want to know how many stalkers hunt their victims down and attempt to murder them. Some succeed, too," he said, grimly.

"I still don't know enough about you."

"By now you should realize that I'm only interested in your safety. You don't have to worry about me trying to seduce you. I prefer tall brunettes with long hair." Clay's discerning glance traveled from the top of Marisol's short blond-streaked hair, down her petite body to her coral-lacquered toenails.

His comment about her lack of height and short hair rattled her. "I'm sure you're very busy as security supervisor. Why should you stay here if you find me so unattractive?"

"I didn't say you're unattractive, just not my type. I'll stay the night because it's my job and you need an able bodyguard."

"Bodyguard? You don't even have a weapon!"

Clay's lips lifted into a humorless smile. "Trust me, I don't need one."

Marisol eyed him nervously. "Maybe I should be afraid of *you!*"

Clay scoffed. "Don't be ridiculous. Tomorrow you can have a double bolt lock installed for your doors."

She sighed deeply. "I'll be all right. You don't have to worry about my safety." With the threatening messages and the strange gift, Marisol knew she would never be able to sleep from worrying about someone trying to break into her apartment. However, having this arrogant, albeit competent man as her bodyguard tonight was out of the question.

She would take his advice and have a double bolt lock installed tomorrow. For now, she'd labor to conquer the fear mushrooming inside of her. She glanced at Clay, inflexible in his belief that she should accept his offer. It would be so much easier to give in and let him protect her, just for the night.

Marisol's mind ticked off the many reasons she knew he was trustworthy. Alan had said Clay was hired to beef up security. He was the best, with many years of experience to back him. Clay's low, gravelly voice was nothing like the high-pitched nasal one on most of her messages. And he had been sitting in her salon when she had received the phone call from the man who had sent the flowers, and had been sitting with her when she had just now received another call and package. Besides, instinctively, she knew Clay wasn't a pervert. Far from it!

Marisol narrowed her eyes. His remark about preferring tall brunettes with long hair had cut deeply and she wasn't going to let him off easily. "For your information, I've never cared for *older,* dark men myself, since my taste is for the blond surfer type. So you're safe from my advances too, Blackthorne." She began to clear the table with short, jerky movements to discourage any further conversation.

"You're foolish not to take me up on my offer."

"You're probably right. I'm sure I'll be extra safe now that I know your preferences."

"If I had known you'd take that comment so personally, I wouldn't have said it." His tone held a hint of mild amusement.

Marisol shrugged and managed a smile. "Forget it. I'm just not used to your blunt style." Reluctant to end the evening and face a night alone in her apartment, she glanced at Clay's beeper and hoped it wouldn't go off any time soon.

She accepted Clay's help in clearing the table and quickly loaded the dishwasher. Her telephone rang again and she intercepted it before Clay could answer.

"Bitch. I know you're not alone. Get rid of him. NOW."

The blood drained from Marisol's face as she slammed down the receiver. In that split second, she blurted out, "I've changed my mind. You can stay and protect me tonight."

"Was that him?" Clay demanded, dialing *69 to trace the number.

Frantic, Marisol nodded.

"Damn it. Whoever called was able to trip up the call return identification service. Why haven't you bought a caller ID system?"

"I did, but when he called, he was able to block it. So I gave the machine to my nail technician, Trini, who needs it to avoid phone calls from her ex-boyfriend." Quaking inside, Marisol forced her trembling limbs to carry her to the bedroom closet where she gathered sheets and a pillow. She brought them to Clay, stacked them in his arms, and turned to leave.

"If I don't go to bed, I'll be worthless tomorrow." She picked up her discarded high-heeled sandals and retreated into her bedroom, firmly shutting and locking the door behind her.

Alone in the living room, Clay attempted to make a comfortable bed out of the sofa. He plopped down and lay back with his arms folded behind his neck. It was only nine-thirty and he was restless.

If he had been home, he would have been studying for the bar exam. His background as a detective investigating some of the most heinous crimes in Miami, both undercover and in the narcotics unit, had propelled him toward becoming the best damn prosecuting attorney in Miami. The fact that he was starting much later than most law students didn't matter. He'd studied criminology before.

Clay heard Marisol in the next room as she prepared for bed. The shower turned on for ten minutes, followed by the whirring sound of a hair dryer. Then silence. He wondered what she was wearing and how she looked scrubbed clean of makeup. Was she wearing a silk nightie or dressed in a T-shirt and panties? Either way she was too desirable. He punched the pillow when he realized he was getting aroused just thinking about her. Damn, but she was a powerful distraction.

Clay hadn't been able to reach Marcos by telephone earlier and now it would be impossible to call him. Tomorrow would be soon enough to report his progress. After fifteen minutes of contemplating his next course of action, he heard the sound of a television behind Marisol's closed door. He glanced at the television set in front of him, but decided against watching it. It was too early for the news and he wasn't in the mood for an inane sitcom. He noticed a few fashion magazines and *The Miami Herald* in a large straw basket, but he decided to forego reading.

Closing his eyes, he realized he'd had a long day. It felt great simply to lay back and rest. He tried to fight the drowsy feeling overcoming him, but he eventually dozed off into a deep sleep.

Clay awoke with a start and checked his watch. Ten-thirty, and Marisol's television was still on. Wide awake now, he suddenly felt thirsty. Walking to the refrigerator, he realized Marisol had abruptly ended dinner after he had insisted on staying the night. He had been dying for coffee, but she had cleared the table in a snit after what he had said about preferring tall women with long, dark hair. He had lied, of course. Marisol's short, tousled hair turned him on, and he found himself fantasizing about nibbling on her soft nape. Smiling to himself, he poured a glass of iced tea and walked back to the living room.

Crossing the living room, he knocked on Marisol's door. "Hey, are you awake?"

"I am now," she called back in dulcet tones.

"Do you have any books or magazines I can read, other than the ones in the basket?"

"There are more magazines inside the wicker trunk beside the sofa."

"OK." Clay returned to his spot on the couch and looked inside the trunk. Beneath the beauty and hairstyle magazines were an assortment of business magazines, *Fortune, Money* and *BusinessWeek*. Just as he reached for the *BusinessWeek,* darkness engulfed the room. Clay froze and concentrated on adjusting his eyes to the sudden blackness. Ears cocked, he listened intently. No sound came from Marisol's room. Concentrating on the shapes in the living room, he crept to the sliding-glass doors leading to a small balcony. He peered outside and noticed that the whole building appeared to be in darkness.

Clay reached Marisol's bedroom door in seconds. "Marisol!" he called. Silence on the other side of the door. She couldn't be sleeping already. He knocked on the door. "Marisol!" Still no answer. He tried the door handle, only to remember that she had locked the door hours earlier.

"Open the door!" Clay felt the hairs on the back of his neck stand on end when she didn't respond. He backed up, prepared to charge toward the door with all his weight. Just before bashing down the door, he tried one more time. "Marisol! Answer me!"

A jolt of fear wracked her body as Marisol listened to Clay banging on her door. She should never have let him talk her into spending the night at her apartment. She berated herself harshly for her impulsiveness. Every time she did something impetuous, she seemed to get into big trouble. But this was the worst! What if Clay was a con artist? He had convinced her that he wasn't the stalker with Alan's assurances that he was the new security supervisor.

He and Alan could be in cohoots! Another man had called her at the salon today while Clay was waiting for his haircut. That could have been Alan! What if Clay was armed with a knife or a gun? She broke out into a cold sweat when she remembered his boast, *"Trust me, I don't need a weapon."* What had he meant by that? Too late, she realized she had never asked for his identification, and only because Alan had said he could be trusted.

Adjusting to the darkness, Marisol's eyes strained to make out the shapes in her bedroom. With a plan of action, she tiptoed to the door.

Just before he lunged at the door, Clay heard a distinctive click signal the door was being unlocked from Marisol's side. He reached down and withdrew the semiautomatic 9 mm. Beretta strapped to his ankle. Gripping it with his left hand, he turned the doorknob with his right.

"Come in," Marisol called out with an exaggerated yawn. "I must have dozed off."

Handgun drawn, Clay entered the room. Instantly, a strong electrical current jolted his body. He lost consciousness and toppled forward like a palm tree felled by lightning.

Three

Marisol's heart slammed against her chest when she saw the gun in Clay's hand. The large flashlight she held wobbled in her hand as she pointed it toward where he lay facedown on the carpet. Transferring her stun gun to the hand that held the flashlight, she carefully removed Clay's pistol from his grip. She darted to her bed and placed it there. Leaping back to his side, she withdrew his wallet from his back pocket and aimed her flashlight at his identification.

A police I.D.!

Relief washed over her. At least that meant he wasn't the stalker. Or was he? she wondered, panicking. It could be a fake I.D. Marisol debated what to do: call the police and ask for information regarding Clay, or call Alan downstairs and have Clay physically removed. The second option seemed the most sensible, except that now she was afraid she couldn't trust Alan either. But if she had Clay thrown out, she wouldn't get the answers she needed from him. While she stewed over her options, the power came back on and he began to stir. She grabbed his gun. It wavered in her shaky hands while she aimed it at him, waiting for him to regain full consciousness.

After several moments, Clay leaned on his forearms

and lifted his body to a sitting position. "Put down the gun," he rasped, the veins in his corded neck straining.

"Not until I get some answers," she said.

"If you can't control the shake in your hands, then slowly, very slowly, put the gun down on the bed. Then I'll answer your questions."

"You can start by explaining your police I.D. As far as I'm concerned, you've lied to me all evening. And there's nothing I hate more than a liar!" Marisol waved the gun at Clay. "Security specialist for this building. Hah!"

"Put down the gun, Sunshine, unless you mean to use it. Otherwise, let me warn you that I can arrest you for threatening an officer with a loaded firearm."

Marisol placed the gun beside her and snorted when she heard Clay harshly expel his pent-up breath. After the scare he'd given her, it was gratifying to see him unsettled. She crossed one leg over the other and folded her hands on her lap. "Well? I'm waiting for an explanation."

Clay rubbed his face. "Yours is not the only case of this kind being investigated. We've received several complaints from other women being harassed like you."

"Really? So why didn't you admit you were a policeman from the beginning?"

"All I can tell you is that I've been assigned to your case undercover." *Now that's not a lie,* he thought.

"Oh, that's nice," she said, looking at Clay in disgust. "All along I thought you were interested in getting to know me. I want you to leave now."

"I can't. I feel like hell." Clay scowled at her. "Where did you get the stun gun?"

"Guess."

"Big brother?"

Marisol widened her eyes melodramatically. "Wow, you're a good detective!"

Clay's features hardened. "I'm the best there is."

She raised her brows at his arrogance. "So why didn't you come straight out and tell me who you were?"

"I just told you—I'm supposed to be working undercover. I needed you to trust me first to gain your confidence."

Marisol breathed out in a loud whoosh. "Well, I guess that's the first honest answer you've given me all day." She looked down and realized that she was only wearing a Miami Dolphins football jersey, which barely covered her bikini panties, and white cotton socks. She glanced at Clay, and their eyes instantly locked, his dark with stark desire, hers bright with surprised arousal. Her breath caught in her throat when she saw Clay's smoldering gaze, proof that he'd taken in every inch of her skimpy attire.

"Turn around," she commanded.

Clay's dimples deepened into an infuriating grin. "It's too late for formality now."

"Not for me it isn't. Now turn around so I can put my robe on."

He reluctantly obliged by turning his head.

Marisol reached for the closest robe in her closet. "You can turn around now." She had grabbed a short, purple silk kimono, a recent birthday gift from her staff at the salon. She had just pulled the edges together and tightened the sash when she heard him emit a short bark of laughter. "What?" she asked, defensively.

"Somehow that robe doesn't seem to match the football jersey and cotton socks." A wry smile tugged at Clay's lips as he shook his head. "This is going to be one helluva case."

Marisol tensed up, not pleased to be the subject of his amusement. "And just what does that mean?"

Clay's dark eyes regarded her with a bemused expression. "You're full of surprises."

"Oh." For once Marisol didn't have a rejoinder. "I guess this hasn't been a very good night for you either. How do you feel?"

Clay stood and reached for his gun, immediately strapping it to his leg. "Better. My strength is back." Taking Marisol's hand in his, he said, "Let's go to the living room where we can talk."

A tingle spread up her arm, and her stomach fluttered from the feel of his warm hand covering her cold one. Every cell in her body responded to his lithe, powerful touch as she followed him into her living room. Releasing his hand, Marisol sat across from Clay. "I suppose you've already guessed that I thought you were the one tormenting me," she said, feeling a little sheepish.

"Something like that," he replied dryly.

"Well, it's your fault," Marisol said, pointing her finger at him. "While I was lying in bed, I started to have second thoughts about letting you spend the night. Then when the power went out, I imagined a scene from *Psycho.*" She didn't appreciate the cynical face Clay made at her statement. "If you'd been honest with me from the beginning, I wouldn't have used the stun gun on you and . . ."

"Forget it," he cut in. "I'm glad to see you have some form of self-defense. You've gotten too many threatening messages today. You need my help."

Marisol crossed her arms and glared at him. "Explain how you happen to be renting a condo in this exclusive complex if you're not the security manager. You certainly told a lot of white lies, Detective."

"The police department arranged it. Others in this area have also been receiving anonymous phone calls," he lied.

"Why didn't I hear about this?"

"We didn't want to cause you further alarm." His solid frame leaned forward on the couch. "I'll spend the rest of the night here guarding you. Tomorrow, I'll investigate where those satin handcuffs were purchased and who sent them to you."

"What if the power goes out again? Do you think there might be a connection to whoever is following me?"

"Could be. I'm going to call Alan and check if the whole building was affected," Clay said, heading toward the kitchen phone. A few moments later, he returned. "The whole building was out of power, not just your apartment."

"I hope it doesn't happen again," Marisol said.

"Don't worry about that. I have excellent night vision."

"Is there anything you don't do well?" She asked flippantly.

"Yes. I seem to have a hard time convincing a little Venezuelan girl to follow my advice," he replied.

She suddenly saw red at his macho comment. "Don't ever call me a little girl," she warned, anger flaming inside her. "I might be small in size, but I'm twenty-nine and sick of being treated like I were twelve!"

He extended his hands and raised and lowered them a few times. *"Calmate, calmate."*

"I don't feel calm."

"Look, I'm sorry I offended you, but you've got to start listening to my advice."

"If I decide to let you continue on this case, you'll

take orders from me, not the other way around!" she said, rising abruptly.

His eyebrows shot up at her militant stance.

Before he could respond, Marisol surprised him by softening her tone. "I'm going back to bed. I didn't sleep very well last night and I'm exhausted. Tomorrow I plan to wake up at six to go to the gym before I open the salon."

"Good. I'll go to the gym with you, and you can make sure to let your friends know you're involved with me now."

She quirked an eyebrow. "Aren't you overstepping your role as bodyguard?"

"The sooner the word spreads that you have a boyfriend, the safer it will be for you until I can get some answers." His implacable gaze challenged Marisol to object.

She sighed, knowing she had no choice but to go along with him for now. "I see your point, but I'm not happy about it."

"There's another problem we have to work on."

"I dread asking what that is."

"You're too trusting," he stated bluntly. "You should have checked me out further before letting me spend the night here."

"Now you're upset I trusted you?"

"You need to be much more cautious. Anyone is a suspect until I rule him out."

"Don't expect me to change my lifestyle just for your investigation," she warned.

"We'll talk about that tomorrow morning," he replied.

Marisol suddenly felt weary, and arguing with Clay held little appeal. She decided to make amends since he seemed determined to protect her. Standing on tiptoes, she lightly kissed his cheek. "Thanks for worrying about me. You're sweet." From his sharp look, it was obvious that he wasn't used to being called sweet.

Clay cleared his throat. "I'm just doing my job."

Marisol smiled at his gruff tone. "I know." Head held high, she headed toward her room.

"Wait a minute," Clay said, passing in front of her. "I need to check out your bedroom." He entered and examined the sliding-glass door. It was securely bolted. Not only did she have it locked, but she had placed a piece of plywood in the tracks to prevent it from being moved. Turning to her, he eloquently arched one heavy brow.

Marisol smiled. "Are you satisfied I take the necessary precautions?"

"Yeah. Good night." Clay strode to the living room and reclined on his makeshift bed.

Marisol regarded him for a moment, then closed the door and locked it. She flung off her robe and climbed into bed. The peck she'd placed on Clay's cheek had been innocently given, but she could still feel his warm skin beneath her lips, and his intoxicating male scent lingered in her memory. She had kissed the sexy groove beside his mouth and now, just remembering the intimacy of it sent little tremors of excitement coursing through her.

She had to admit that Detective Clay Blackthorne was the most formidable male she'd ever met. Why wasn't he married at his age? He was probably divorced, she decided. Marisol had dated many men since moving to Miami, but nobody like Clay. He was tough, yet gentle, and his personality was so intense, so compelling, that she found herself anticipating the challenge of making him lighten up. His dimples were devastating, and his smoky, deep voice, especially when he called her Sunshine, made her tingle straight down to her toes.

Marisol silently chided herself to stop behaving like a teenager with a first crush. Switching off the lamp on her nightstand, she flopped over onto her stomach and snuggled her face into her goose-down pillow. When she closed her eyes, Clay's handsome image appeared clearly, a welcome change from the disturbing dreams she'd been having lately.

By six-fifteen the next morning, Marisol was dressed and ready for her workout. After brushing her teeth, she glanced in the mirror and groaned. Without makeup, she looked about fifteen years old. She brushed her hair and fluffed it, then quickly applied black mascara to darken her light brown lashes, and put on coral blush and lipstick.

When Marisol walked out of her bedroom, she caught a glimpse of Clay on her lanai. Barefoot, and dressed only in black jeans, he exuded fluid strength in every well-honed muscle of his body. Marisol stared, transfixed by the play of muscles in his tanned back as he went through several T'ai Chi exercises. He was pure masculine grace—lean, bronzed and skilled. He was not overly built, but his body was lithe and lean, corded with powerful muscles.

Clay turned to the right, pivoted on his right heel and moved his left hand down in front of his stomach, palm upward. He shifted his body to the left and turned at the waist, simultaneously moving his left hand diagonally across his torso to his left shoulder. At that moment he looked up and caught Marisol

watching him. For several moments, she just stared
into his fathomless black eyes, mesmerized by his potent male presence. They broke eye contact when Clay
reached for his black polo shirt. Marisol was disappointed that she had only caught a glimpse of his
beautifully sculpted chest. By the time she reached the
patio, Clay was wearing the shirt.

"You didn't have to stop because of me," she remarked, controlling an urge to smile.

"That was the last exercise I do with my medita-
tion." He glanced at her gym attire. "Give me ten minutes to run to my apartment and change into gym
clothes so we can leave."

"What about breakfast?"

"I'll grab some orange juice at home."

Clay breathed a sigh of relief when he reached his
apartment. That was a close call. If Marisol had seen
his bare chest up close she would have noticed the
serpent tattoo that started on his left shoulder and followed a path to his heart. No doubt she would have
made the connection between him and Marcos. He
and Marcos had identical tattoos, resulting from a
night of too much hard liquor and two playful women.
Fifteen years earlier, the women had taken Clay and
Marcos, two drunken students, to a tattoo parlor and
cajoled them into having serpents etched on their
chests. Clay had since settled down from those wild
days, and so had Marcos, but the serpent was there to
remind him of his reckless youth.

Once he changed into gym clothes and packed a
change of clothes for work, Clay returned to Marisol's
apartment.

"Are you planning to shower and change at the gym?" Clay asked.

"I wasn't planning to. Normally I come home first."

"Pack what you need so we can leave for your salon together."

Marisol's eyes narrowed. "You can't possibly be planning to play nanny to me at the salon."

Clay leaned back to caustically observe her. "Do I look like Mary Poppins to you?"

Marisol giggled at the image. "So you're only going to escort me to work?"

"That's right. Now let's go."

Marisol gathered her makeup kit and a change of clothes, then headed for the gym with Clay. In the parking lot, Clay's eyes automatically gravitated to Marisol's sultry stride as she walked ahead of him in snug bike shorts. He clenched his jaw to stop the immediate rush of hot desire.

He cleared his throat. "Marisol, I've been meaning to talk to you about your walk."

Puzzled, she turned to him. "What about my walk?"

"It's too sexy."

"What are you talking about?"

"This," Clay said, mimicking her walk. Hips swaying, he walked in a swish-swish rhythm as he tossed his head and lifted his chin.

Marisol burst out laughing. "You missed your calling, Blackthorne. With those lean hips and that walk, you should be on the catwalk doing runway modeling."

Clay frowned. "This isn't a joke. Your walk draws the type of attention you can't afford right now."

Marisol scoffed, "I've never heard that complaint from anyone else."

"Trust me, it's true."

"It's too bad you feel that way, because my walk is natural, not something I work at and can change on a whim." Marisol's green-flecked hazel eyes flashed with a spurt of anger. "I didn't move away from Marcos to have another man dictate to me. I'm insulted that you think I walk like this to attract attention."

"I didn't say you do it on purpose. Just modify it. It's my job to protect you."

"Yeah, right," she muttered.

When they reached the entrance, Marisol sauntered toward the locker room, leaving him behind. "I'll see you on the floor," she called out. "Tae Bo class starts in five minutes if you want to join me."

Clay nixed the class, instead keeping a watchful eye on Marisol from the office while he spoke to the receptionist. He asked for, and received, a computer printout of the male members who had come in that morning. When the class was over, Clay hung around the juice bar and watched Marisol through a glass wall as she talked with several men in the free-weight room.

It was obvious to Clay that he wasn't the only man who found her attractive. Marisol was too damned cute for her own good. Her smile was infectious; her friendliness, irresistible. And unfortunately for Clay, she was also an outrageous flirt! His mouth tightened when he saw one of the bodybuilders reach over and pat Marisol's back. She said something to him and they laughed together. Clay decided Marisol had spent enough time socializing. If he didn't intervene, that ape would soon have his paw on her again.

Clay walked up to them and placed a possessive arm around Marisol's waist. "Let's go, *Nena*," he said, emphasizing the endearment.

Marisol gave Clay a forced smile. "Oh, hi. I was wondering where you'd gone. Guys, this is Clay, my boyfriend. Clay, this is Joe, Tony, and Julio."

"Hi," Clay responded gruffly, giving Marisol's waist a slight squeeze. "Let's go."

"Sure." Turning to her friends, she said, "'Bye, see you guys on Friday." Once out of their sight, she shrugged Clay's hand off her waist and walked ahead of him toward the locker room. She turned to glance at him. "I can be ready in half an hour. How about you?"

"Ten minutes. I'll read the paper while I wait."

A half hour later, showered and dressed for work, they headed for the parking lot where Clay instructed Marisol on safety precautions to follow throughout the day. "I need a complete list of the men who have been to your beauty salon this past month. Also, try to think of anybody you might have snubbed who would want to get back at you."

"That's almost impossible! There are lots of guys whom I've dated only once and haven't wanted to see again. Problem is, I can't remember all of them."

Clay stared at her incredulously. "Are you telling me you randomly date anyone you want and don't remember their names?"

"Don't give me that look, Blackthorne. I don't go on that many dates. Sometimes, when I'm itching to dance, I go nightclubbing with Trini, the manicurist who works for me. She's had a really rough time getting over her break-up with her boyfriend, Ray. Since she loves to dance as much as I do, we've hit a few salsa clubs in South Beach. But any date I've been on, I've always insisted that the guy meet me where we're going," she said. "I always pay my own way the first time, so he can't make any demands on me." Marisol felt that sounded cautious and reasonable enough.

"Have there been any demands anyway?" he asked.

"That's none of your business."

"It is now."

Marisol shrugged. "If I don't like the guy, I don't give him my phone number. Since moving to Miami, I haven't invited any of my dates back to my apartment." She would have done that only if it had been a serious relationship, and that had been lacking in her life since Gustavo. "Listen, I'm not a floozy, but I'm no hermit either. I enjoy meeting people and going to parties."

"Well, Sunshine, you can kiss your party days good-bye."

Her mouth dropped at his inflexibility "What do you mean?"

"I mean you'd be asking for trouble if you went to a South Beach nightclub alone or even with your manicurist friend, now that this guy is obsessed with you. Try to think of anybody who's come on to you after you've said 'no'."

"There were several persistent ones, but I think we parted as friends."

Clay looked up at the sky as if to summon patience, then back at her. "Get me a list of your male salon clients by this afternoon. We'll go over it after dinner tonight."

Marisol's face lit up with interest. "We're having dinner together?"

"Yeah. I'll make stir-fry," he said.

"You're kidding."

"I never kid."

"No kidding."

Clay's seductive, deep-set eyes regarded her steadily as he ignored her teasing remark. "Do you own a wok?"

"'Fraid not."

"We'll improvise. I'll be at your apartment at seven-thirty tonight. In the meantime, here's where you can reach me if anything comes up." He handed her a paper with a phone number jotted on it. "Until tonight, Sunshine."

"Qué chévere!" Marisol said, thrilled that Clay would be cooking a meal for her. The only thing marring his invitation had been his commanding tone. She'd have to remind him that she took orders from no one but herself. First her walk, and now her social life. What else would he attempt to change?

Marisol shook her head as she got into her red convertible. She turned on the radio full blast and drove to the salon with Clay's car trailing behind hers. Glancing in her rearview mirror, she made eye contact with Clay and gave him a sassy wink.

Late that afternoon in her salon, Marisol massaged the small of her back with both hands and sighed. It had been an exhausting day. One of her clients had come in to complain about her highlights. Her husband hated the way she looked as a blonde and she wanted her money back. A model with baby-fine hair came in insisting on a layered haircut that would only work on someone with thick hair. When Marisol had tactfully explained that her hair was not the right texture for that cut, the young woman had made a scene and accused her of being rude.

"Sometimes this job can really get to you," Marisol muttered, stifling a yawn. It was ironic that she hadn't slept very well the previous night knowing Clay was in the living room. She should have felt safe and secure with him as her bodyguard, but instead, he had invaded her thoughts and dreams with his enigmatic presence.

"I'm glad that I just work here as a manicurist. I don't know how you can be so polite to these people when they're rude to you," Trini said. "You should just tell them to bug off."

Marisol studied Trini. Every week Trini had a different hairstyle or hair color. This week it was platinum blond, which created a startling contrast to her olive-toned complexion. Trini's lips were lined in a deep wine shade and filled in with rose-colored lip gloss. Because of her exotic Venezuelan beauty, Trini could get away with her funky style. She was skilled as a manicurist, but Marisol had also hired Trini because her offbeat look added to the ambiance of the salon that catered to many fashion models and actors living in South Beach.

"It's called survival," Marisol replied, in answer to Trini's previous question. "I'm determined to give John's salon a run for his money. I want to make this salon a success, no matter who's against it."

Trini's brown, almond-shaped eyes widened. "Who would be against it? You can't be talking about John Cippino!"

"Of course not, silly. We're friends. Besides, John already has the big-name celebrities coming to him. I'm talking about our dear landlord." As soon as the words were out, Marisol regretted them. There was no sense in alarming Trini about her job. She had just broken up with that loser, Ray, a month ago and had been depressed ever since. Marisol was glad Trini had finally left him, especially when the last beating he administered landed her in the hospital. She hadn't had the heart to tell Trini that Ray had been at the salon recently, flirting with everyone there while he asked about Trini.

To reassure her, Marisol said, "Don't worry. I can handle Mr. Guitierrez even though he wants to practically double my rent when I renew my lease. He says he already has a client lined up for this space."

"Who?"

"He won't tell me, but I don't think he's bluffing."

"What a rotten deal! What are you going to do, *chica?* Why don't you ask that gorgeous big brother of yours for help?" Trini looked down at her sculptured nails, studying the eggplant-colored polish.

"You know I would never go to Marcos for something like this! I'm going to fight back with some legal advice from an expert."

Trini looked up with interest. "Who? Lawyers are expensive."

"Not this one. He just graduated from law school and hasn't taken his bar exam yet. I'm sure I can get him to read my current lease as a favor to me. Then I'll know how to fight Mr. Guitierrez."

Trini's eyes gleamed with interest. "Have I met this guy?"

"I gave him a haircut yesterday. I don't know if you remember him, but he was tall and lean, with a dark tan and gorgeous black hair."

Trini let out a whoop of delight. "I know exactly who you mean. A real hottie!" she exclaimed, fanning herself. At Marisol's chuckle, Trini crooned, "He was sooo fine! What a difference from all the *papi chulos* I've seen at the clubs lately. I've been meaning to ask you what his name is so I can call him."

"Not this one, Trini. He's all mine." Marisol laughed at Trini's crestfallen expression. "When I get to know him better, I'll ask if he has a friend for you."

Trini flashed a naughty smile. "You're on, *chica.* I want one exactly like him."

As she drove home, Marisol looked forward to Clay's meal. No man had ever cooked a meal for her, not even Gustavo.

Arriving at her apartment door, she stopped dead in her tracks when she saw a dozen bloodred roses lying in an open long white box on her doorstep.

"Read the card," a male voice rasped behind her.

Four

Marisol reacted instinctively, lunging backward and stomping hard on his instep with her spiked heel. She heard several items hit the floor before she whirled around.

Clay clutched his foot and hollered, "Yeouch!" He lost his balance and fell forward, tumbling them both to the floor. The length of his hard body covered hers and their faces were inches apart.

"You scared the living daylights out of me!" Marisol exclaimed breathlessly.

"I just asked you to read the message," he murmured, staring at her mouth.

"Did you send those roses?" she demanded.

"Of course not." His gaze flickered to her eyes, then returned to her mouth.

Marisol's pulse quickened. Clay looked intent on kissing her and nothing in the world could make her stop him. "Your deep voice startled me," she said, expelling her breath.

"It's the only voice I have. By now you should know it." Clay's mouth descended upon hers without further hesitation. His lips pressed against hers firmly, with a hunger so intense it sent a ripple of pleasure coursing through her. She melted beneath his searing kiss, allowing Clay to mold his lips to hers, loving the way he slid his tongue across the seam of her mouth, beseeching entry. When his tongue touched hers, a flood of lust swamped her loins. Clay intimately explored the inner recesses of her mouth until she was breathless and reeling with pleasure.

Shifting slightly, he slipped his arm beneath her shoulders and caressed her cheek with his other hand, holding her face steady as he made love to her mouth. Marisol's whole body quivered and a delicious heat spread through her limbs. Not wanting it to end, she kissed him back hungrily, her small body pressing against his larger one.

Vaguely aware of groceries scattered around them, she only felt his muscled chest pressed against her aching breasts and his hard thigh resting between her tender ones. She had never been kissed like this before, so confidently, so thoroughly; she was lost to everything but Clay's potent sexuality. Marisol closed her eyes and savored her pleasure. When he lifted his lips from hers, she blinked, frustrated by the jarring loss. Speechless, she watched his jaw tighten while his mouth formed a resolute line.

His face flushed darkly, Clay gritted his teeth and looked like he was fighting to regain his composure. "Are you all right? You look like you're going to pass out."

Marisol's senses hummed with desire. Wasn't it obvious how much his kiss had affected her? Her breath locked in her throat when she attempted to speak. Clay had pulled back after giving her that dizzying kiss and now she didn't know what to make of it. Slowly, she exhaled and managed to say, "I'm OK. You're just a little heavy for me."

Clay shifted his weight off her and rocked back on his heels to squat beside her. He refilled the bags with groceries while Marisol adjusted her clothing. Placing the box of roses atop the groceries, he stood up and said, "Open the door. My foot is killing me."

Feeling a little guilty, Marisol stood and smoothed her clothing. "I guess I stomped on you a little too hard. Sorry." She opened the door for Clay and watched him limp inside. Marisol's pulse still pounded from his hungry kiss as she followed him on wobbly legs. "Put the bags on the kitchen counter and I'll get an ice pack for your foot."

"Now I know the real reason you wear high heels. Who taught you a move like that?" he asked, eyeing her shoes warily.

When Marisol didn't answer right away, he let out an exasperated sigh. "Let me guess. Big brother?"

She grinned at him and nodded.

"I have to hand it to him. Your brother has taught you well. You're not only self-sufficient, you're damn near fearless!"

While he massaged his instep, Marisol filled the ice pack. "Sit here," she said, motioning to the bar stool at her kitchen counter. She placed the ice pack on his injured foot.

"Do you relish humbling me?" he asked sternly, quirking one dark eyebrow at her.

She tried to hide a grin. "I don't know what you're referring to."

"Yes, you do. First the avocado beauty treatment, which I hardly enjoyed; then you knock me to the floor with your stun gun, and now you practically fracture my instep. I'd rather not know what else you're planning." His gruff voice was a mixture of mild annoyance and resignation.

Marisol giggled softly. "Leave it to me. I guarantee you'll be surprised."

"Ay," Clay groaned as he held the ice pack pressed to his foot. "Read the note on the box."

Eyeing the card nervously, Marisol sighed. "I guess I can't put it off any longer." Anxiety gripped her as she opened the small white envelope and pulled out the card. In her haste to hand the note to Clay, Marisol dropped it and they bumped hands as they both reached for it. She felt the fine black hairs on the back of his hand and goose bumps spread up her sensitized arm. She was reminded of Clay's powerful body intimately pressed against hers in the hallway and her breath quickened.

Clay took the card from her and read it out loud.

"Marisol, why are you cheating on me? You two-timing whore. Stop being a tease. You're going to marry me. ONLY ME. Get rid of him or I will."

Clay's jaw tightened as he swore under his breath. "Check your answering machine."

Marisol forced herself to play back the messages and felt vast relief that there were no weird messages. Suddenly weak, she sank into a chair. "Well, what do we do now?"

Clay seemed to measure his words when he said, "We eat first, and talk about this later. I need to put this problem on the back burner while I cook."

"How can you be so calm after somebody's threatened our lives?"

His solemn gaze rested on her. "I'll watch over you. I won't let anyone harm you."

"Thank you," Marisol whispered, inordinately pleased by his answer.

Clay's expression lightened, captivating Marisol with a hint of his deep dimples. "Now, where do you keep your frying pans?"

Marisol reached in the cupboard and handed him a new large Teflon skillet.

His mouth quirked up at one corner. "Haven't had much use for it, have you?"

Marisol shrugged. "I told you I wasn't much of a cook."

"That's OK, Sunshine, because I am," he said with supreme male confidence. He handed her the raw vegetables. "Here, slice these. I'll peel the shrimp."

"And I thought you were going to do all the work," she teased with a little pout.

"Get working," Clay ordered in a mock stern voice. He gently clasped her waist and turned her toward the counter.

Marisol grabbed a kitchen towel and put it around his waist. Tucking the edges of the towel into the waistband of his black pants, she fought the urge to wrap her arms around him and lean her cheek against his broad back. He smelled heavenly.

Clay turned his head and glanced down at her. "Thanks," he said. His dark gaze locked with hers briefly before he turned back to the shrimp.

A delicious shiver tickled her spine. "My pleasure," she replied shakily. "I'll make rice." She poured water, rice, and salt into her rice cooker, then sliced the vegetables in silence. She couldn't seem to keep her eyes off Clay's strong hands as they peeled the shrimp. She was suffused by a sudden urge to run her hands over his, feeling the warmth and texture of his smooth brown skin.

"What are you looking at?" he asked.

"Your hands. When did you learn T'ai Chi?"

"Shortly after I turned ten."

"It's an unusual martial art form for a small child to be interested in," she observed.

"After Dad died, my mom remarried and we moved to a small town. Mom enrolled me in T'ai Chi because even though I was a skinny runt, I usually ended up in a fist fight when provoked. Unfortunately, that was often."

"Why?" she asked, puzzled. From what she had observed about Clay, he seemed very controlled, not only his temper, but other emotions as well.

"A group of kids used to make fun of my baby brother because he's mentally handicapped. It would really burn me up, so I used my fists a lot. My mom hoped the T'ai Chi class would teach me better discipline and self-control."

"Did it?"

"You bet." Clay shrugged his broad shoulders. "But I still won't tolerate anyone treating my brother, Jimmy, with anything less than respect. He's my one soft spot."

Marisol would have liked to ask more about his childhood, but Clay's expression stopped her cold. She wondered at the look of raw pain that shadowed his face before his eyes turned hard and devoid of emotion. There was no sense in asking questions about Jimmy when Clay looked like he already regretted divulging his one weakness.

"The shrimp are ready now. Stand aside." Clay dumped the shrimp into the sizzling peanut oil and seasoned them while he stir-fried. When they turned pink, he emptied them into a bowl and stir-fried the Oriental vegetables. He tasted a snow pea. "Perfect." Returning the shrimp to the frying pan, he added dry sherry. Instantly, a delectable aroma arose from the pan. "Here have a taste." Clay speared a juicy shrimp and blew on it before he fed it to her. "Careful, it's hot."

She moaned in appreciation. "Mmmm, *qué rico!* Let's eat."

Marisol set the table and together they polished off Clay's meal. She patted her lips with a napkin. "That was the best shrimp I've ever eaten. Where did you learn to cook like that?"

"From a beautiful Japanese woman I dated a long time ago. I picked up some recipes just watching her prepare terrific meals for me."

He sounded like he was used to having women cater to him, Marisol decided, not pleased by the revelation. She also didn't care for his mention of the beautiful woman.

"What's for dessert?" he asked.

"Mint chocolate-chip ice cream. Want some?"

"Sure and a cup of coffee. That is, if you don't mind too much," he replied dryly.

Marisol harrumphed, remembering the other night. "Of course I don't mind. I only mind making you coffee when you say you're only attracted to tall brunettes with long hair."

The dimples beside his hard mouth deepened slightly. "Did I say that?"

"Yes. I know my stun gun didn't give you amnesia, too."

"I only made that remark because you'd just admitted to being sensitive about your height. If you thought I wasn't attracted to you, you wouldn't worry that I might make a pass, instead of protecting you." His gaze swept over her with a look that made her insides flutter. "Truth is, I find you adorable."

Marisol gulped as she watched his eyes darken with passion. "You do?"

Clay nodded, reached over to stroke the tiny cleft in her chin with his thumb, then placed his hands around Marisol's waist and pulled her onto his knee. "You definitely appeal to me," he murmured, gently tilting her head forward to stroke the downy blond hair at her nape. He deposited soft, warm kisses along her neck, leaving goose bumps to form in their trail. Placing his hands on either side of her face, he kissed her deeply, covering her mouth with his as he slid his tongue inside.

Marisol snuggled against him, aware of the difference in their bodies, how her round bottom and soft thighs contrasted sensually to his hard thighs. Jarred by the realization that she wanted to remain on his lap, she moved to disengage herself. "You're distracting me from serving dessert," she said softly.

"Dessert can wait." With a deep, sexy growl he reached for her again.

"But I can't wait." Jumping up from his lap, she moved away from his reach.

Clay followed her into the kitchen. "What's wrong?" he asked, his voice gruff.

She bit her lower lip and avoided his searching gaze. "You shatter my self-control."

"Yeah, likewise," he said, his strong hand gently cupping her jaw.

"But you're supposed to be my bodyguard, not my lover," she said, almost choking on the last word. "Things will only get complicated if we get any closer. You saw what that guy wrote in the note. He threatened your life! Doesn't that worry you?"

"No. My life has been threatened before. You're the only one I'm concerned about, Marisol." Clay pulled her toward him. "You can trust me. I'll protect you with my life if necessary."

Overwhelmed by his impassioned words, Marisol gazed into his intense, glowing eyes. "I believe you would."

The telephone rang causing Marisol to jerk away from Clay and reach for the phone.

"Let me answer it," Clay said, snatching the telephone from Marisol. She wasn't surprised when he handed her the phone. "He says he's your brother."

Frustrated by the interruption, she held the receiver to her ear. "Hi, Marcos, why are you calling?"

"What kind of a welcome is that for your favorite brother?" Marcos inquired.

"You mean my only brother." When Marcos started to protest, she said, "Just kidding. It's good to hear from you. What's up?"

"I wanted to know if you've had any more mystery calls or flowers."

Even though he tried to keep his voice light, Marisol knew Marcos too well and she could detect his concern. "Not since the last time we spoke. But I did report it to the police and there's a detective working on the case. So you can stop worrying about me and get on with your life."

"A detective? You went to the police about this? What else has happened?" he thundered. *"Vale, mocosa,* if you're keeping something from me, I'll never trust you again."

She *hated* when he called her a brat. "Don't be an

idiot! If you'll stop sputtering, I'll tell you. When I contacted the police about the phone calls and flowers, I was surprised to find out that other women in this building were having the same problem. A detective was already assigned to this case undercover."

"Really? What's his name?"

"It's nobody you know," she replied, not wanting to give him the opportunity to get in touch with Clay.

"OK," Marcos said, his tone resigned. "Well, I'm glad you had the sense to call the police. Take good care of yourself and keep me posted."

Marisol loved Marcos and knew he meant well, but she couldn't help resenting the way he constantly told her what to do. "Don't worry, I'm in good hands," she said, winking at Clay. "I'll keep in touch. Thanks for calling."

Marisol hung up the receiver and turned to Clay. "I knew Marcos would check up on me this week. Maybe now that he knows you're involved with this case he'll relax."

"Why did you downplay the danger?"

"Because if Marcos even suspected things have gotten worse, he'd come here in a heartbeat and try to take over. Worse still, he might tell my parents! That's just what I want to avoid."

The phone call seemed to trigger a change in Clay's previous amorous mood. Marisol watched him walk stiffly toward the living room. "Why don't you relax on the couch while I change clothes?"

Clay nodded absently, not meeting her gaze. Shortly afterward, she returned to the living room wearing an orange tank top, tucked into a pair of khaki shorts. She sat down next to Clay, who was examining the note she'd received that evening with the flowers.

"Where do we go from here?" she asked.

"I'll take this note in and have the police lab assess it along with the other ones. Where's the list of your male clients at the salon? I need to cross-reference it with the list of members I got from the gym."

Marisol reached for her purse on the coffee table. She retrieved the list and handed it to Clay. "Here."

"Have you fired anyone this year who might have been coming on to you?" he asked, studying the list.

"No. There was only one stylist I had to let go. He was unreliable and I heard from a friend that he was doing crack. Anyway, it couldn't be him. He's gay."

"What's his name?"

"Nicholas Ferrer."

"Did you call a locksmith today?"

Marisol grimaced and snapped her fingers. "I knew I forgot something. It was such a hectic day, the only thing that kept me going was thinking about the dinner you promised to cook for me."

"I'll have double bolt locks installed on your front door and extra locks on your balcony sliding glass doors. I'm spending the night on your sofa until those locks are installed," he said.

"That's fine with me. I can't imagine why you'd want to spend another uncomfortable night on a sofa, but I will feel safer if you're here tonight." She kicked off her sandals and curled her legs under her on the sofa.

Clay picked up the remote control from the coffee table and flicked on the television. "Let's watch the news."

Marisol fell asleep next to Clay as they watched the evening news program. When he noticed her nodding sleepily, he stretched out on the sofa and tucked her into his side, adjusting her head so that it rested beneath his chin. Gently, he stroked her silky, tousled hair and rested his chin against it. Lying beside him, her petite, delicate frame appeared vulnerable, almost fragile, and Clay was tormented by an overwhelming need to keep her safe from harm.

She was now his to protect.

Clay shut off the television and settled more comfortably, with Marisol's delectable body snuggled against him. He closed his eyes and smiled regretfully, looking down at her hand where it lay on his shoulder. Marisol was such a temptation! But Marcos's phone call had served as a reminder that he was relying on Clay to protect his little sister, not seduce her. The last thing he wanted was to ruin his friendship with Marcos by taking advantage of his kid sister.

Clay reminded himself that he must remain impersonal. But everything about Marisol invaded his senses—her baby-soft skin invited stroking and her fragrant scent made him want to inhale deeply, filling his being with her feminine essence. In vain, he tried to think about something else until he finally managed to fall asleep with her cuddled in his arms.

Marisol was the first to stir. Her mouth felt parched and her lids heavy as she strove to crawl through the honeycombs of lethargic sleep. She attempted to stretch only to find she was solidly pressed against something hard. Looking down, she saw a large, brown hand curved over her hip. She couldn't remember how she'd gotten into that position, but a lusty shiver vibrated through her body when she realized it was Clay who held her. Glancing up, she caught him watching her with heavy-lidded eyes.

Marisol rubbed her eyes. Was she awake or still dreaming? *If this is a dream, please God, let it continue,* she requested silently. Clay's warm touch convinced her that she wasn't dreaming. She had actually fallen asleep in his arms after only knowing him two days! When she glanced down quickly to check if all her clothes were intact, Marisol felt Clay's chest rumble. She pushed back from him to see his face clearly. He was chuckling.

"What's so funny?" she asked.

"You." He nudged the top of her head with his chin. "You look like a contrary kitten with its fur rubbed the wrong way."

"And you look like a jungle cat ready to pounce," she countered. "What time is it?"

Clay glanced at his watch. "Five o'clock."

"No wonder I'm still sleepy," she complained, yawning. She stood up and stretched. "I'm going to bed. Do you want a pillow and some sheets?"

"No. I'm going out to the lanai to meditate."

She made a face to show what she thought of his plans. "At five in the morning?"

"I've slept enough. I feel refreshed now." Clay rubbed Marisol's shoulders. "You go on to bed. I'll wake you up at six."

"Thanks." Even though she'd just slept more deeply than ever, she still felt the need for another hour of sleep. Marisol didn't bother changing clothes. She slipped off her sandals and lay down on top of her comforter, instantly falling asleep.

True to his word, Clay walked into Marisol's room at six. She was lying on her side with her face resting on her hand. He stood beside Marisol and patted her shoulder. "Wake up, Sunshine. It's six o'clock."

Marisol opened her eyes and yawned. She tried to focus her gaze on her watch. "Already?" she grumbled.

He nodded. "I've never seen anyone sleep so deeply."

Clay's thick black hair was still damp from his shower. He had changed into faded blue jeans and a black T-shirt. She blinked when his hard mouth quirked up at the corners and the lines beside it deepened into sexy grooves. He was giving her a smile that reached his wonderful eyes.

Unsettled by his potent male presence, Marisol shot up from the bed and rushed to the bathroom. "I'll be out of the shower in a minute and then I'll fix us some breakfast." Without waiting for his response, she showered and shampooed her hair, then dried herself quickly. She pulled on snug blue jeans and a salmon-pink blouse that tied at the waist. Her wet hair wrapped in a towel, she walked into the kitchen.

Clay sat on a stool at her kitchen counter, watching the morning news on her small portable television set and looking very much at home. His presence filled her kitchen. Powerfully male, he tempered strength with steadfast protectiveness when he was with her. Just thinking about the way she'd fallen asleep pinned against his side made her legs go weak.

"Good morning." Leaning over to kiss his freshly shaven jaw, she murmured, "Mmm, you smell great. Like you've been walking in a green forest after the rain."

"That's pretty poetic, Sunshine. You smell like a fresh-squeezed lemon," he said, patting her hip.

She flushed at his familiar gesture. "It's my special brand of shampoo. It's all—"

"I know, I know," he interrupted with a wry face. "It's all-natural."

"You can scoff all you want." Marisol's face lit up with mischief. "You have to admit your hair looked beautiful after the conditioner I put in."

"Don't remind me of that mess," he warned. "You'll ruin my appetite."

Marisol giggled. "What do you want for breakfast? Mashed avocado with eggs?"

"Come here, smart aleck," he said, grabbing her hand to pull her toward him.

She danced away from his grip. "Does *café con leche* and tostadas sound OK?"

"Sure."

"Let me get the paper first." She walked to the front door and opened it. When she pulled the newspaper out of the bag, a card fell out. She forced herself to read the note out loud as she returned to the table.

"Bitch. I'm tired of being nice. Stop shacking up with that bastard. You're going to marry ME, only me. Then, I'll punish you for this. I'm getting turned on thinking about it."

"Oh, my God," she moaned.

Clay swore profusely. The thought of Marisol being threatened by some pervert made his skin crawl.

"He's really getting nasty!" Marisol said, sickened by his sadistic message. "What am I going to do?"

Clay clenched his teeth and it was several moments before he spoke in a controlled tone. "I might have a temporary solution. Let's have breakfast first while I plan how we're going to thwart him."

Despite the sickening knot in her stomach, Marisol brewed espresso and steamed milk for the *café con leche.* She sliced several cold oranges and used her juicer to produce a frothy pitcher of orange juice. By the time she finished, the toast was ready. She placed everything in front of Clay, feeling proud of herself for producing such a nice meal. Making breakfast had somewhat calmed her, but she dreaded reading the note again.

"Great orange juice," Clay said, downing the contents of his glass.

After some hesitation, Marisol cleared her throat. "Clay, about last night . . . Why did you let me sleep on you that way? You should have woken me up."

"You were out cold. Besides, you're so light, I could barely tell you were there."

"Right," she drawled. "And you're so quiet I could barely tell you were there." She sighed. "I hate not knowing what's going to happen next. It doesn't seem like this guy's going to give up easily. I'm not used to having to watch over my shoulder constantly, and I don't like having to depend on you to protect my life."

"Right now you have no other choice."

Marisol grimaced. "Just knowing that this guy is affecting my lifestyle makes me so furious. I've been managing very well on my own—until now."

"Don't underestimate him. I can't begin to tell you the despicable things men like him have done to innocent women. Rape, even murder. You have to be one step ahead and street smart, Marisol, or you'll get hurt." After a pause, he added, "I've decided on a plan where I can watch you around the clock and keep you safe while I find the stalker."

"What is it?" Marisol's coffee cup stopped in midair as she waited to hear Clay's answer.

"You have to trust me and believe that I'm proposing the best course of action."

Marisol groaned. "I don't think I like the sound of that."

"Promise you'll go along so I can protect you completely."

"What are you talking about? How can I possibly promise until you've told me what you're planning?" Marisol asked, wanting to clobber him for being so obtuse.

"Since he's so obsessed with marrying you, we'll beat him to it." He regarded her with that no-nonsense look she recognized too well. "We're getting married today."

Marisol's coffee cup slipped from her hand and clattered to the table, splashing coffee everywhere. Jumping up, she clutched a handful of napkins. She wiped the spilled coffee from the counter and inadvertently knocked over Clay's mug, sloshing hot coffee onto his lap.

"Hey!" Clay yelled, pushing his stool back from the counter.

"I'm so sorry!" She grabbed more napkins and blotted the tops of his jean-clad thighs. With a groan, Clay seized her hand before she reached up any further.

"Leave it. It'll dry," he uttered in a strangled voice.

She anxiously eyed his crotch for damage. "Did I burn you?"

"No, it wasn't that hot." Clay let out an exasperated sigh. "Relax, Sunshine. It's OK."

"I can't relax! Especially after your little joke about getting married."

"It was no joke. I meant it."

Marisol watched the corners of Clay's hard mouth

lift into a half smile and her attention focused on his eyes. They were dead serious. If he only knew how many times she had daydreamed about marriage. She was twenty-nine, not a spinster exactly, but at an age where getting married and having babies held much appeal.

Marisol slumped onto the bar stool, feeling as if the air had been knocked out of her lungs. She took several deep breaths to compose herself and buy time.

"Do you always propose to the women you protect?" she asked.

"No. You're the first," he replied. "I have to jump the gun on this guy. He's determined to marry you, and says so in every note he sends. If we're married before he can get to you, it will either discourage him when he finds out I'm a detective, or it will make him come forward. And if he does, I'll be right there waiting for him."

"Why can't we just live together?" she asked lamely. "I'll tell everyone you're my boyfriend and my bodyguard."

"Being married is a helluva lot more permanent than shacking up with someone." Clay observed her with keen eyes as he awaited her answer.

"Then we'll just pretend that we're married."

"That would never work. This guy is so obsessed with marrying you that I'm sure he would need evidence to believe we really got hitched."

"Why would you be willing to give up your freedom for me?" She cocked her head to one side and waited for his answer.

Clay shrugged. "It's only temporary. I don't like to see an unprotected woman being terrorized. Particularly someone as naive as you."

"I am *not* naive," Marisol protested, indignant that

he would think so. "And I'm *not* going to marry you, Blackthorne!"

Despite her retort, Marisol was intrigued by Clay's marriage offer, even if it was offered for reasons other than love. He had promised to guard her with his life. No man had ever said anything so generous to her, nor so noble. Even though he had lied to her initially about his job, she understood why. Marisol believed in him. He was a man with a strong character and a sense of honor, whom she could respect, and that alone made him special. She smiled inwardly. If her situation hadn't been so desperate, this would have been quite tempting.

She was too honest to deny the strong physical attraction between them. She could feel the heat in Clay's dark, hooded gaze whenever he looked at her. He was so controlled and self-confident, a man who must have lived a dangerous life, replete with women and adventure. His hot, hungry kisses the previous evening had left her breathless, craving more. She wasn't sure how much longer they could remain platonic if they lived together.

"Say yes, *Nena*." Clay's husky voice beckoned her from her reflections.

"No, I can't," she said, trying not to be persuaded by the endearment he'd used.

"We need to be together as much as possible. The stalker has access to this building. Anytime now he might make a real move for you."

"I'll have to think about it. In the meantime, we'd better hurry and get to work," she said, not wanting to dwell on the enormity of what he'd just proposed.

*   *   *

At the salon, Marisol glanced at her watch. Two o'clock. If she hurried, she'd be able to run some errands before going home to prepare a special meal for Clay. Hastening to her car, she had to leap backward when a silver van backing out of a parking space almost hit her.

"Watch where you're going!" she shouted, shaking with anger. When the driver stuck his hand out of the window in an obscene gesture and tore out of the parking lot, Marisol felt fury at her powerlessness that very moment surge through her. That jerk could have killed her, or at the very least crippled her. She looked up at the sky and noticed ominous purple clouds gathering on the horizon that threatened a drenching storm. Hoping to avoid it, she hurried to the supermarket.

Once home, Marisol unpacked the groceries, avoiding the message light that blinked on her answering machine. Just as she was putting the orange juice in the refrigerator, the phone rang.

"Luz was hit by a car in the parking lot!" Trini cried when Marisol answered the call.

Fear wracked Marisol's body. "How badly was she hurt?"

Trini's voice quivered. "She's still unconscious. We're waiting for the ambulance to arrive."

"I'll be right there. I'm leaving now."

Marisol rushed to the salon. In the car, she wondered about the coincidence that she had also almost been hit by a van in the parking lot that very day. It had either been a woman with very short dark hair or a man driving. That's the only thing she'd been able to tell from the back of the driver's head. She couldn't tell if it had been a man's hand or a woman's that had gestured from the van window.

When Marisol arrived at the salon, the ambulance was already there. Two paramedics carried Luz, pale and unconscious, into the ambulance. Trini rushed to Marisol's car before she could get out.

"Will she be all right? What did the paramedics say?" Marisol asked.

"She's in shock," Trini said. "I think a van backed up and hit her from the side as she was walking to her car."

"Are they taking her to Mount Sinai Hospital?" Marisol asked.

"Yes. Her doctor will meet her there."

"I'll drive behind the ambulance and call you from the hospital."

"OK. Don't worry, Marisol," Trini said in a reassuring voice.

Marisol nodded, then willed her hands to stop trembling as she drove toward the hospital. By the time the ambulance arrived at the emergency room, Luz had regained consciousness. She was rushed inside for further tests. Marisol waited in the lobby and glanced at her watch repeatedly, unable to block out the terrifying thought that Luz could have been killed.

Hours later, when Luz was finally released from the hospital, Marisol insisted on driving her home.

In the car, Luz's shoulders were slumped and her face looked chalk-white as she asked, "Can you take me to my parents' house? They live in Hialeah."

Marisol squeezed Luz's hand. "Sure, no problem. Are you OK?"

Luz nodded. "I'm just a little shaky still." Her eyes filled with tears. "It terrifies me that I remember very little about the accident."

Marisol's heart went out to her. "You've been

through a lot. Were you able to get a glimpse of the person who hit you?"

"Not really. I know it was a man, but I can't remember his face. All I remember is being hit by the van and then waking up in an ambulance."

"Did you notice the make or color of the van?"

"It was silver, but I don't know what make or year it was."

"Silver?" Marisol paused a moment to collect her composure. The van that had almost hit her earlier that day had been silver. It wouldn't do to tell Luz that she suspected the hit had been planned for herself. "Trini said there were no witnesses to the accident. Not even the lady who found you lying in the parking lot could give the police any details."

"Who would do something like that?" Luz asked.

Marisol's heart ached hearing Luz's tremulous voice. "I've never understood hit-and-run accidents. Leaving an injured person unaided is so cowardly, it's obscene."

After getting directions to her house, Marisol pulled into Luz's parents' driveway twenty minutes later.

"Thanks for the ride home," Luz said gratefully. "I'll be at work tomorrow."

"If you don't feel well, call me in the morning. I can make other arrangements so you can have more time to recuperate."

"OK. Thanks again."

"You're welcome." She waited until Luz entered the house before driving away.

When Marisol pulled into her building's parking lot she was filled with a sense of impending doom. Her mind was preoccupied with Luz's accident as she leaned against the elevator wall and waited for her floor. She had called Clay earlier at the precinct and explained that she was at the hospital waiting for the results of Luz's tests. After voicing many objections, Clay had reluctantly agreed not to go to the hospital and that he'd meet her at her apartment instead.

As he drove to Marisol's apartment, Clay's mind was burdened by the news of Luz's hit-and-run accident. His gut feeling was that it had been no accident. He'd noticed on several occasions how much Luz resembled Marisol from a distance. But up close they looked quite different. Luz had an offbeat style, with three holes pierced in each earlobe and dramatic eye makeup reminiscent of the sixties. Yet the similarities were strong enough for someone to mistake them, especially someone intent on harming Marisol.

The stalker was a formidable opponent. So far, he'd covered his tracks, but Clay was determined to catch him soon, and when he did, he'd make damn sure Marisol was never threatened again.

When he arrived, Marisol flung open the door. "Thank God you're here!"

He pulled her into his arms and stroked her tousled hair. "Are you OK, *Nena?*"

She pulled away and led him to the answering machine. Punching the button, she said, "Listen to this."

Clay heard the familiar voice of the stalker. He sucked in his breath, feeling as if he'd been kicked in the gut. Slamming his hand against the counter top, he punched the rewind button and listened again. Burning wrath singed through his veins like acid at the message: "I told you to get rid of the cop. Luz's accident was a little lesson for you. Next time, you won't be so lucky."

Marisol clutched her hands together. "I don't know how much more of this I can take! Poor Luz. The stalker attacked her just to terrify me. I was nearly hit by a van backing out of the parking lot earlier today, too!"

Clay stood still and stared at her with hard eyes. "Why didn't you tell me that when you called from the hospital?" he spat out.

"My only concern at the moment was for Luz. I planned to tell you later."

Clay's steady black gaze held hers. "Do you understand now why we need to get married?"

Marisol kept silent.

"If you agree, the marriage will be in name only. As soon as I arrest him, you and I get an annulment. Deal?" He held out his hand for a shake.

Marisol lifted her chin and ignored his proffered hand. Why would he think she might want anything else? "*If* I agree to marry you, the annulment follows as soon as the stalker is caught."

Clay's laugh was too cynical for her liking. "Good. By then you'll be happy to be rid of me. I'm definitely not marriage material. I plan to keep my vow never to remarry."

Clay's challenge only served to fuel Marisol's energies. So he thought he wasn't marriage material, did he? "All right," she agreed, feeling better than she had all day. Being around Clay always made her feel safe.

"What time do you open the salon tomorrow morning?"

"Ten o'clock. Why?"

"I want to get the marriage license and have the ceremony performed as soon as possible." Clay walked into the living room as if the decision had been made.

Marisol gulped. "So soon?" Frantically, she searched for a good reason to postpone their marriage, but came up empty. "My first appointment is at eleven." She sighed. "I guess I can call and have Trini open for me. She has an extra set of keys."

"Perfect. I have to go to my place and pick up some clothes."

Clay left Marisol's apartment and immediately called Marcos to report his progress.

"I didn't ask you to marry her, Che," Marcos said. "Just protect her."

"Trust me, I know what I'm doing. Her situation is getting more complicated. *Tu hermanita* needs a full-time bodyguard."

"De acuerdo. But how did you get *her* to agree?"

"I assured her that as soon as the stalker is caught, we'll get an annulment. You know how I feel about marriage."

"Yes, I think you've told me enough times," Marcos said, chuckling. "Marisol must trust you a lot if she agreed to a marriage of convenience. Remember, don't tell her you're working for me."

"OK, but I'm beginning to hate this charade. I'll continue for her sake. And yours," Clay said. "I'll call you tomorrow."

"All right. I'm counting on you to watch over Marisol. Don't let her get hurt—in any way," Marcos said meaningfully.

Five

The following morning Marisol answered Clay's knock on her bedroom door, amazed that he'd dressed up for the occasion. She took in how handsome he looked in the white dress shirt with a gray and black silk tie, and black linen slacks.

"You look beautiful," he said, his gaze sweeping over her knee-length, sleeveless linen dress. "Your skin looks golden against the white dress."

"Thank you," she said, flattered by his compliment. "It was the most conservative outfit I could find for a wedding."

Clay tugged at the tie he didn't seem comfortable wearing. "Let's go, Sunshine."

Everything happened too fast for Marisol. In less than an hour they bought their marriage certificate and for under a hundred dollars they were married in the same office. What a staggering difference from a real ceremony, especially if she had been married in Venezuela, where a wedding was the social event of the year. She looked down at her hand. Clay had used his mother's ring for the ceremony— on loan.

Marisol bit her lower lip to keep from weeping. She tried to tell herself that she was being a dope, that those things didn't matter. When everything was resolved, they would be annulling the marriage anyway. But none of those rationalities helped. The truth, plain and simple, was that she was a hopeless romantic who had promised herself a sumptuous wedding celebration someday, not some depressing ceremony performed by a bored clerk.

Marisol glanced out of the car window and watched the fat raindrops plop against the glass pane. It had even rained today. She remembered hearing somewhere that rain on your wedding day meant good luck. But not even that superstition could lift her spirits. Her eyes filled with tears and she mournfully sighed out loud.

Clay turned to glance at her. "What's wrong?"

With chagrin, Marisol dashed away the self-pitying tears that were sliding down her cheeks. "Nothing," she replied with false brightness, keeping her face turned away from him.

Pulling off the busy highway, he eased the car over to the curb and shut off the engine. He gently turned her face toward him. "You wouldn't be crying if nothing was wrong." His hand cupped her chin as his thumb slowly stroked its cleft.

"I feel so foolish," she mumbled.

"Why?" he asked, pained by her sadness. He was so used to seeing Marisol confront everything with optimism that her tears were his undoing.

"I know this isn't a real wedding, since it's only temporary, but I always dreamed of something different," she said wistfully, wiping at her tears.

"What did you dream of? Tell me," he coaxed, his hand stroking her smooth cheek.

Marisol smiled through her tears, tilting her face as she looked off dreamily. "I imagined a church wedding, filled with all of my family and friends wishing me luck, and a man I adore standing at the altar, promising to love me forever. Later, there would be a wonderful party with all the trimmings—champagne, music, and lots of flowers." She peered at him with misty eyes. "I'm sure that sounds pretty ridiculous to you."

"Shh, *Nena,*" Clay crooned, overwhelmed by the need to kiss her and make love to her until she cried with joy, not sadness. He held Marisol's face in his hands and kissed her tenderly, then pulled away, lest he give in to that yearning. Her words had touched something locked deep inside of him, feelings that he kept guarded and never allowed to surface. He wanted her to have everything she had dreamed of. But he knew with a rough certainty that he could never be that man standing at the altar, promising to love her forever.

"One day your marriage will be like that. But for now, we need to keep you safe," he said, resolutely closing his heart to tender feelings.

Clay tore his gaze away from Marisol and pulled his car out into traffic. It felt like a knife was twisting in his gut; he didn't want the longing to love and be loved in return by Marisol. He didn't want to feel that vulnerable ever again. Someone like Marisol would want children along with marriage, and Clay had long since written both things off. The brutal betrayal of his ex-wife, Jillian, who had aborted their child without his knowledge, was painful enough to last a lifetime. Jillian's reasons had been so heinous, he didn't even want to think about them. Clay's trust in marriage, or any woman's promises thereafter, had been destroyed.

When Clay and Marisol arrived at the salon, they ran inside to avoid the pelting rain. Smiling broadly, Marisol announced their wedding and watched her employees' reactions, which ranged from surprise and shock to elation. They were hugged and congratulated by everyone in unison. Luz snuck out and returned with two bottles of champagne and a vanilla frosted cake.

Shortly after they toasted, Clay turned to Marisol. "I have to leave now. I'll come by at seven and we'll celebrate tonight." He leaned down to whisper in her ear, "Cancel your appointments for tomorrow. We need a full day together." To everyone's delight, he gave Marisol a lusty kiss. Cheers of encouragement followed him out the door.

"Marisol, you're blushing," Trini teased. "Why didn't you tell me you were getting married? I thought we were close."

Marisol winced at the hurt in Trini's voice. "We are close, Trini. It just happened so suddenly! I can't believe I got married either, but I'm crazy about Clay. There's a lot more involved here. We'll talk later," she promised, feeling guilty about shocking poor Trini with her news. She was probably bemoaning the fact that she was the only single one now, since Marisol's best friend, Nuri, was away on her honeymoon.

"Where did you get your dress? I love it," she said, hoping the compliment would bring a smile to Trini's dejected face.

"Thanks! I designed it," Trini boasted, brightening a little.

Clay sat at his desk with a crime sketch in front of him, trying to analyze it for the third time. He let it slide from his hands onto the desk. It was useless. He'd sworn he would never remarry and today, with a five-minute ceremony, he had changed everything. What had possessed him to marry Marisol, even as a pretense? Before meeting her, no amount of gratitude to anyone, not even Marcos, could have made him get married, even if it was in name only.

Since divorcing Jillian, Clay had retreated into a solitude he had come to cherish. Independence and T'ai Chi, along with his close bond with his brother, Jimmy, had been his only weapons to combat the anguish he had experienced after Jillian's selfish abortion. A year had passed before Clay even began dating again, but he still hadn't healed from Jillian's treachery. It had hurt more than any wound he had ever suffered in police work. It had crushed his soul.

Clay could feel the subtle changes creeping into his life. He was plagued by the sudden realization that he relished being in close quarters with Marisol. Ever since she had entered his life, she had illuminated his dark soul. Her feminine, romantic ideas of a perfect wedding had warmed his heart more than he cared to admit. But he knew he wasn't the man of her dreams. His life had been too gritty, his outlook too dark. He would only make her despair over his views on marriage and having children. Hell, the wall around his heart suited him just fine.

Detective Jenny Wilkins walked into his office carrying a Styrofoam cup filled with steaming Cuban espresso coffee and several tiny plastic cups that resembled thimbles. The statuesque, green-eyed brunette poured the strong brew into two cups.

Clay downed his cup like a shot of whiskey and handed it back to Jenny for a refill. "Aah," he groaned. "How did you guess I needed that?"

"I took one look at you," she replied. "I've known you too long not to figure out something big is going on." Jenny looked him over with a quizzical grin. "What's with the fancy duds?"

Clay glanced down at his clothes. He loosened his tie and tugged it off. "I got married today."

Jenny's mouth gaped as she stared at him. "Did you just say you got *married?*"

Clay nodded. "You can close your mouth now."

Jenny whistled softly. "I didn't know you were serious about anybody. Who's the new bride?"

"Marcos Calderon's younger sister," he replied. "You remember meeting Marcos, don't you?"

"Of course." She grinned and wiggled her eyebrows. "How could I forget him? Dr. Calderon is not somebody you forget." She sank into a chair across from him. "Out with it, Clay. I want the full story."

Clay chuckled mirthlessly. Jenny had often tried to set him up with her friends in the hopes that he would change his negative opinion about marriage.

"Marcos asked me to watch over his kid sister, Marisol, as a favor to him. Some guy is stalking her anonymously," Clay said.

"That's it?" Jenny stared at Clay in disbelief. "That's why you married her?"

"I feel strangely protective of her," he said. "The phone calls and gifts he sent her were getting kinky.

I'm convinced this guy means to hurt her. He's obsessed with marrying her—writes that in every note. Our marriage should discourage him long enough for me to find him."

"Sure, and I have a property in little Haiti to sell you," she said, with a knowing grin. "Come on, Clay. We both know that marriage won't stop a psychopath."

"Maybe this guy's not a psychopath and just some loser I can scare off." He added emphatically, "It's only temporary. After I arrest the stalker, we're getting an annulment."

"Not planning to consummate this marriage, are we?" Jenny chortled. "Marisol *could* change your views about marriage."

"Don't you have work to do?" he demanded, irritated by her amusement. He stalked out of the room, certain that Jenny was still smiling a goofy grin.

Caramba, were all women such romantics?

The afternoon rain had finally cleared when Clay returned to the Villabella Salon. Marisol's breath caught in her throat when she saw him standing in the doorway, his rigid, muscular physique partially blocking the afternoon sun's rays filtering in behind him. Dark sunglasses shaded his eyes and his hair was combed straight back from his face, emphasizing his sharp cheekbones and chiseled jaw. All lean muscle and sinew, Clay emanated a predatory aura of magnificent animal grace.

Marisol's palms began to perspire and her mouth went dry. She fumbled with her purse, dropping it as she tried to retrieve her keys and lock her salon.

"Ready to leave?"

Clay's deep voice created tremors in Marisol's already wobbly limbs. She remembered the way he kissed and a shiver of excitement wracked her body.

"I just have to lock up," she replied, dismayed when her voice came out in a squeak. She turned off the lights and closed the salon door. Making an effort to smile at Clay serenely, she inquired, "How was your afternoon?"

"Not as productive as I'd hoped. I don't have any definite leads on your case yet, but I've been checking and cross-referencing the lists you gave me. The satin handcuffs you received weren't purchased at any local store in Miami-Dade County. I'm still trying to trace them."

"Oh," Marisol said, disappointed, as she walked beside him to the parking lot.

Clay opened the car door for her. "Did he try to contact you today?"

"No, thank God!" Marisol touched his arm lightly. "Do you mind if we stop at Publix before we go home? I need to buy a few things."

"No problem."

At the supermarket, Marisol and Clay picked up a loaf of bread, cheese, eggs and fresh fruit. As Clay maneuvered the shopping cart into the shortest lane, Marisol stopped him.

"Not that one," she said, turning the cart away.

"Why not?"

"There's someone I want to say 'hi' to. I'll be right back." Clay nodded, then stood at the end of the line, absorbed in *Newsweek,* while Marisol walked to the front of the register to her favorite bag boy.

"Hi, Jimmy. How's everything?" she asked. She was glad that Publix had a policy of giving mentally disabled people the opportunity to bag groceries. Marisol had met Jimmy on the first day he started work, and during the past year they had become friends.

Jimmy's face crimsoned and he ducked his head. "Hi, Marisol," he said, in his slightly slurred speech.

"Why are you working so late?" she asked. "It's seven-thirty."

"I work the afternoon shift now. I'm going home soon," he said slowly.

"How are you getting home?" she asked, concerned because it would be getting dark soon.

"The bus."

"Come with me," Marisol said, leading Jimmy by the arm to where Clay was bent over unloading the groceries. "Clay, I'd like you to meet a good friend of mine. This is Jimmy. He's at the end of his shift and I'd like to offer him a ride home."

Looking bewildered, Jimmy scratched his head. "Hi, Clay, how do you know Marisol?"

Clay gave him a puzzled look. "I should ask you the same question, Jimmy. Why are you working so late?"

Marisol gawked at them. "You two know each other?"

"Jimmy *es mi hermanito*," Clay explained.

"Your little brother?" Marisol repeated. She recovered graciously. "In that case, you'll have to join us for dinner, Jimmy."

Clay put his arm around Jimmy's shoulder. "How about it? Would you like to have dinner with us?"

"Sure," Jimmy said, turning an even brighter shade of red.

Marisol observed Jimmy's open face, filled with adoration for Clay. It was obvious that Clay was Jimmy's hero and that he was happy to be included in their plans.

They dined al fresco at La Palma Restaurant among softly lit potted palm trees and pale ocher arched columns. Seated intimately around a candlelit table, Clay, Marisol, and Jimmy spent an enjoyable evening, keeping the conversation light and focused on Jimmy.

As they were leaving the restaurant, Marisol's heart lurched when she glimpsed the broad back of a man ahead of her. She could have sworn it was Gustavo. He had the same cocky swagger and expensive Italian cologne. It was ridiculous to be annoyed that Gustavo was out of his usual South Beach turf and in Coral Gables, but a mere glimpse of him was enough to irritate her. When he briskly entered a red Porsche and sped away, Marisol shuddered, then rubbed her bare arms.

Clay placed a protective arm around her shoulder and murmured in her ear, "Is something wrong?"

Marisol tried to dispel her apprehension by smiling at Clay and Jimmy. "No, nothing. Why?"

"You looked a little rattled."

Marisol forced a laugh, dismissing Clay's concern. There was no use telling him that she thought she had seen Gustavo. Marisol knew that if she mentioned seeing Gustavo, Clay would suspect him of being the stalker. The thought was preposterous. Her ex-fiance was too self-confident to remain anonymous while he sent her gifts and notes. And the voice on the phone had not been Gustavo's.

"I guess I'm a bit jumpy," Marisol said, linking her arm with Jimmy's.

It was amazing how Jimmy didn't resemble Clay in the least. The only similarity between them was in the dark hair, although Jimmy's was a shade lighter, and much finer than Clay's coarse hair. Jimmy was plumper and considerably shorter than Clay and had a sweet, boyish face with round brown eyes.

Glancing at Clay, she noted there was nothing sweet or boyish about his features. Clay's rugged face held testimony of hard living and survival. More than once, Marisol had seen a glimmer of pain shrouded in Clay's watchful eyes.

Clay drove Jimmy to The Haven of Hope, a special working community for mentally handicapped adults. When they arrived, Marisol said good-bye to Jimmy. Her heart soared as she watched Clay walk him to the door, his strong arm fondly draped over his younger brother's shoulders. After they spoke for a few moments, Clay hugged Jimmy and left. A warm glow suffused her being at the love Clay lavished on Jimmy. Someday Clay would make a wonderful father; she was certain of it.

They drove home in silence, each lost deep in thought. When they reached Marisol's apartment, Clay said, "I'll put away the groceries while you pack an overnight bag. I wasn't able to hire a locksmith, so tomorrow I'll install the locks on your doors myself. We're staying at The Delano Hotel tonight."

Marisol raised her brows. "Why not your apartment?"

"Where do most newlyweds spend their first night together?"

"In a hotel?"

"Bingo. If the stalker's watching, we'll be more convincing."

Marisol couldn't argue with that, so she quickly packed and changed into ivory silk palazzo pants and a matching fitted sleeveless vest. She was glad of her choice; the silk was luxurious against her skin, and, after working all day in the linen dress, she felt like lounging in something soft and fluid. Marisol hastened to join Clay. It was already ten-thirty and she was anxious to leave. She walked into the living room, clutching her overnight bag. "I'm ready."

They checked into the hotel as Mr. and Mrs. Clay Blackthorne, with only two small overnight bags, at eleven o'clock in the evening. Marisol ignored the teenaged front-desk clerk who smirked at her knowingly as he handed Clay the keys.

In the elevator, Marisol whispered with a nervous giggle, "I don't think he believed we were married."

"I know," Clay replied, his face darkening with annoyance. "One more smirk from him and I would have taken the boy aside for a little talk."

"Blackthorne, are you for real?" she said, amused by his reaction.

Clay didn't respond to her question. When they arrived at the top floor, he grasped her hand and led her to the penthouse suite.

Stunned, she turned to him. "The penthouse?"

Clay's grin flashed brilliantly against his dark, chiseled face. "After the past two nights, I decided you deserved an evening of peaceful sleep." He unlocked the door and together they entered the most breathtaking suite Marisol had ever seen. Chippendale furniture, Aubusson carpets, crystal chandeliers and exquisite oil paintings surrounded them.

"All these flower arrangements!" Marisol exclaimed happily. "They're gorgeous!" She leaned down to inhale the heady fragrance of pink tea roses.

"Come with me," Clay said, leading her to the bedroom. A round bed stood in the center of the room, with a sheer ivory canopy that hung from the ceiling to form a gauzelike tent. Next to the bed was a small table covered with Battenburg lace. On the table, a chilled bottle of champagne rested in a crystal ice bucket. Beside it, a silver tray bore plump strawberries and a small bowl of *dulce de leche,* her favorite Venezuelan sweet.

Suddenly feeling faint, Marisol sank down on the edge of the bed. This was beginning to feel like a dream. She was with Clay in a penthouse suite that had all the makings of a romantic evening. Yet that very same morning, Clay had assured her that the wedding was in name only. "I thought our marriage was for appearances only. That's what I agreed to this morning," she reminded him.

"I know what you're thinking," he replied. "Relax, I'm not trying to seduce you, Marisol. You were so sad today. I wanted to erase the tackiness of our wedding ceremony."

Marisol was touched by his thoughtfulness. "Thank you," she said. "But where are *you* planning to sleep?"

His mouth curled upward into a sardonic grin. "Since I'm your husband, I'll sleep beside you. Unless you object."

"Of course I do!"

"Why? I promise to stay on my side of the bed."

"Things might get out of hand if we're in bed together."

He lifted a dark eyebrow. "Is that your only objection?"

"Isn't that enough?" Marisol's pulse quickened at the thought of Clay lying beside her in the bed. Even if he remained fully dressed and on top of the sheets, it would be too tempting. But how could she voice further objections, when in all fairness, she should have been the one offering to sleep on the couch?

Her mind made up, Marisol smiled. "I'll sleep on the sofa tonight. After the two uncomfortable nights you've spent on my couch, it's your turn for a good night's sleep."

"Believe me, your couch was a luxury compared to some of the grungy places I've slept while working undercover narc. I'm used to roughing it."

Marisol didn't know how to respond to that. Growing up with more luxuries than she needed, she had never had to rough it. Compared to her cushy life, Clay's world seemed dangerous and dismal.

"There's a guest robe in the bathroom. You can freshen up while I pour the champagne," he suggested.

Marisol glanced around her. "This place must have cost a fortune."

"It's only one night, Sunshine."

Only one night, she repeated silently. A lot could happen in one night!

Marisol carried her overnight bag into the dark green marble bathroom and filled the Roman bathtub with hot water and the freesia-scented bath oil the hotel provided. She stripped out of her clothes and stepped into the fragant steamy bath. Exhausted, she leaned her head back and closed her eyes, dozing off almost immediately.

Marisol screamed when she felt a callused hand grab her shoulder. Opening her eyes, she found herself inches away from Clay, a concerned expression on his face.

"I have never seen such a sound sleeper," he remarked, clearly exasperated. "Didn't you hear me? I knocked on the door several times."

"Get out!" she shrieked, crossing both arms over her exposed breasts. She drew her knees up to hide the triangle of curls directly in his line of vision.

Clay exited the bathroom and plopped on the bed. Frustration burned inside of him as he tried to block out the nude vision of Marisol, lusciously golden from the top of her tousled hair to the tips of her tawny toes. He could still see her pale, pink-tipped breasts tilted upward beneath his hungry gaze. As he waited for her to emerge from the bathroom, his tension mounted, and he tried to erase the seductive image from his mind. He had only gone in to check on her because he'd thought something might be wrong. She'd been in the bathroom for almost an hour, and after repeatedly knocking, he had gone in to check on her.

Moments later, Marisol stormed out of the bathroom, wrapped in the white robe provided by the hotel.

"What's wrong with you? You're acting like a wasp stung your tail," he said, noticing that she looked adorable in the oversize robe.

"I just love sitting stark naked in a bathtub while you stare at me," she said sarcastically.

"I was not staring at you. I already explained why I went in." Clay pointed an accusatory finger at her. "If you didn't sleep like a dead person, I wouldn't have had to open the door in the first place!" he said, defending his honor.

Marisol's eyes twinkled suddenly and she grinned. "You're forgiven."

"I didn't say I was sorry," he reminded her.

"I know, but you should have. I forgive you anyway." She perched beside him on the bed. "Is this for me?" she asked, reaching for a filled champagne flute.

"It was, before you came charging in here. I was planning to toast you."

"Come on, lighten up, Blackthorne. I was embarrassed that you saw me so . . . bare!" She faltered. Marisol spread a little of the creamy, caramel-like *dulce de leche* on a strawberry and popped it into her mouth. "This is sheer heaven. How did you ever arrange to have my favorite dessert here?"

He shrugged, dismissing the thoughtfulness of his gesture. "It wasn't too hard."

She poured herself another glass of champagne and refilled Clay's. Lifting her glass in the air, she said, "Here's to you, Detective Blackthorne. You're more than a bodyguard . . . you're a treasure."

Clay's eyes shimmered like black lava as he gazed at her above the rim of the glass. Lifting it, he toasted, "And here's to you, Marisol. You fill every room with sunshine."

Marisol clinked her glass against Clay's. Her face suddenly felt flushed and her body tingled unbearably. "Thank you," she managed, before closing her eyes and sipping the remaining champagne. Nibbling on a third strawberry, she asked softly, "Did you also arrange for the bouquets?"

Clay's chuckle rumbled deeply through the room. "I guess I overdid the flowers."

"Not at all. They're exquisite," she said, sighing happily. She refilled her glass of champagne and marveled at how delicious it tasted. "I have never felt so pampered."

Clay's warm hand closed over Marisol's before the

champagne flute reached her lips. "Easy on the champagne."

"Spoilsport," she protested, pushing his hand away. "We can't let this wonderful champagne go to waste." Marisol fanned herself daintily. "Do you feel warm?"

"No," Clay lied, loosening his shirt around the collar. Truth to tell, he was hot all over just watching Marisol's moist pink mouth savor the ripe fruit. "Instead of more champagne, have another strawberry."

"I couldn't." Marisol patted her stomach. "I've had three already." Ignoring Clay's protest, she continued to sip the champagne.

Clay's gaze was drawn to Marisol, and he felt like he was drowning in a sea of desire. Her mouth curled at the corners into a seductive little smile and her skin invited stroking. Marisol's catlike eyes sparkled with desire. His gaze returned to her rosy mouth, devoid of lipstick and softened by champagne. Imagining the intoxicating combination of sweet strawberries, champagne, and Marisol's plush mouth, Clay leaned forward for a taste. Her lips were like the softest velvet against his as they parted generously to allow the intimate stroking of his tongue on hers.

The need to touch her soft body consumed him. With near savage urgency, he wanted to see her naked again, to bury his erection deep inside of her pliant body and make her cry out with unbridled lust. Inclining his back against the headboard, he pulled her up beside him. His hand slipped under her robe and rested on her bare thigh as his other hand stroked the velvety nape of her neck. He nipped her earlobe gently.

"I'm wild for you, *Nena*," he rasped softly in her ear.

His husky voice caused tiny shivers to tantalize the nerve endings along her spine. Marisol moaned, dazzled by the onslaught of sensations coursing through her body. Clay's warm hand on her thigh set her aquiver. With half-closed eyes, she kissed the side of his neck.

"I'm wild for you, too," she whispered back. Clay's lips descended on her neck and she whimpered softly. The exquisite sensations his warm tongue elicited were the opposite of anything she had ever experienced with Gustavo.

Marisol languidly stretched against him. "I'm in the most wonderful dream and I never want to wake up. Make love to me, Blackthorne," she cajoled.

Her large hazel eyes sparkled seductively, but Clay reined in his lust when he smelled the champagne on her sweet breath. Although he hadn't had a woman in months—not from lack of opportunity, but from lack of real interest—he felt compelled to stop. Marisol was obviously vulnerable from the champagne, and Clay's conscience surfaced to torment him.

"I can't, *Nena,*" he said regretfully. His brow beaded with sweat as he used considerable self-restraint to remove his hand from her soft thigh before he stroked her legs apart and entered her in one deep plunge.

Marisol kissed his rigid jawline. "Why not?" she asked, gazing up at him. "Don't you want me?"

"More than you'll ever know." His throat felt clogged. "But you've had too much champagne. If we continue, you'll hate yourself tomorrow and I'll hate myself even more for taking advantage of you." He called on all the discipline he had learned to hold himself together.

"You're not taking advantage of me. It's not the champagne that's affecting me; it's you." Marisol placed her hands on either side of his face and her lips moved lightly up, pausing to kiss his cheekbones, then his closed eyes, from his lashes to his brows. Her robe parted and he got a glimpse of her breasts through her sheer camisole before she melted against him. "Make love to me, Blackthorne," she repeated.

Swearing under his breath, Clay rose from the bed and stiffly walked away. "I can't," he muttered, his back turned to her. He was painfully aroused and very close to giving in to her request. Silence surrounded him as he waited a long while until his raging lust was under control. When he turned to face her, Marisol had fallen asleep.

Clay cautiously approached her, glad that she was such a heavy sleeper. He removed her robe and reveled in the tantalizing picture she presented. She lay before him in languid slumber, dressed in a sheer white camisole and short satin tap pants. Clay's finger traced her rosy, swollen lips. His gaze slid over her round breasts down her sweet belly to her slightly parted thighs. Another surge of lust nearly made him wake her up. Snatching his hand back, he drew the sheets over her and stalked to his side of the bed.

He stripped down to his briefs and climbed into bed, stiff with pain. Careful not to awaken her, he smoothed back a silky strand of hair from her face. He only trusted himself to touch Marisol's slender throat, feeling its delicate structure beneath his hand. He yearned to hold her breasts and stroke the tips with his thumbs, to watch her arch her back and whimper as his wet mouth closed over each nipple.

Abruptly, he jerked his hand back and threw his arm over his eyes. He was out of control, damn it! Clay rose from the bed and paced furiously, refusing to glance at Marisol as she slept. He strode to the bathroom and took a long, cold shower. When he returned to bed, Marisol was asleep on her stomach, oblivious to his torment.

His thoughts turned to Marcos and how indebted he had felt toward him ever since he had attended to Jimmy in the emergency room of Jackson Memorial Hospital. Years ago, Clay had rushed Jimmy in during an asthmatic crisis. Marcos had put him on a respirator immediately and changed his medication, and ultimately, his quality of life, encouraging Jimmy to take up swimming to strengthen his lungs.

Clay lay awake for a long time watching Marisol sleep. He flinched when he realized that he had almost given in to her sweet appeal for lovemaking. He had come to cherish everything about Marisol, especially the way she interacted so lovingly with Jimmy. Her affection had been genuine, not condescending, and Clay was touched at the considerate way that Marisol treated Jimmy. In his mind's eye, he remembered Marisol smiling at Jimmy and placing her hand on his shoulder while she chatted with him animatedly. At that moment, he had wanted to share the rest of his life with her. She would make a wonderful mother someday.

God, it hurt to admit that she would have to marry someone else to have children. But Jillian had made him realize that no woman would be willing to have his child with the risk that it would have a genetic defect.

Six

When dawn's first rays filtered through the sliver between the drawn curtains, Clay rose and dressed. He performed his T'ai Chi ritual, then returned to the bedroom to find Marisol still asleep, lying on her stomach in the center of the bed. Sheer ivory gauze veiled her body in a gossamer glow as the white satin molded to her curves like a second skin. Clay took in the way her graceful neck topped an alluring valley that dipped in her spine before reaching the apex of her shapely backside. One leg bent at the knee, she clutched a pillow beneath her, curving her body over it.

Clay's blood heated at the sight, but he forced himself to turn away. He went into the living room and ordered room service. When it arrived, he walked back to the room and touched Marisol's foot to awaken her. When that didn't work, he lightly tapped her upraised bottom. "Wake up."

Marisol buried her face in the pillow and ignored his summons. Another tap, this one more determined, got her attention. She turned over indignantly and sat up. Grabbing the sheet, she pulled it around her and grumbled, "A simple 'wake up, Marisol' will do, Blackthorne." She jumped out of bed and hurried past him to the bathroom. "I'll just be a minute."

"Don't fall asleep, or I'll come in and get you again." He chuckled when he heard her lock the door.

Five minutes later, teeth brushed and face washed, Marisol joined Clay at the small table. She took one look at the scrambled eggs and bacon before her and blanched, quickly covering them up. "I'll just have juice and coffee."

Sipping the orange juice, she felt awkward beneath Clay's steady gaze. Oblivious to her discomfort, he polished off his breakfast with relish. How could he eat like that when her own stomach was tied up in knots? Clay was acting as if nothing had happened last night, and she felt like screaming with frustration. She managed to scald her mouth and throat with a large gulp of coffee.

"Aren't you going to eat your eggs?" he asked mildly.

Marisol shook her head. "My stomach feels a little queasy."

Clay quirked one black eyebrow, lips twitching slightly at the corners. "Too much champagne?"

"Yes, and don't say 'I told you so.' " Marisol's eyes focused on the delicate floral pattern of the coffee cup to avoid Clay's intense gaze. Seconds later, she looked up from her coffee cup and found him grinning openly. For someone so tough-looking, she seemed to easily coax a smile from him.

She wondered how the evening had ended between them since she couldn't remember anything beyond his refusal to make love to her. "Why are you smiling?" she asked, not especially anxious to hear his answer.

"How much do you remember about last night?"

"Enough to be slightly mortified. I should have listened to you. I don't handle champagne very well."

"I thought you handled it beautifully." Clay reached across the table and held her cold, hesitant hand in his warm one. "Don't worry. Nothing happened last night. You fell asleep before I could explain why we shouldn't make love." His brows came together as he regarded her. "One of the hardest things I've ever done was turn away from you last night. But you drank a little too much champagne and I didn't want to take advantage of you."

"I knew what I wanted," she said, refusing to be embarrassed by her honest reaction to him.

"I wanted the same thing, but we can't let that sidetrack us. Your safety is of utmost importance. If we step over the fragile boundary between us, there will be no turning back. We have to stick to business for now."

Feeling miserable, Marisol looked down and set her cup on the table. "I'll shower and get dressed so we can leave," she said, with as much dignity as she could muster. She wouldn't let Clay realize how much his words hurt her. The foolish optimist in her had hoped for more, a declaration of his feelings perhaps. But he hadn't uttered the most important words she wanted to hear, and now she desperately needed to retreat to the bathroom to save face.

Marisol closed the bathroom door and squeezed her eyes shut as she leaned against it. When was she going to learn not to be so open? Why couldn't she have shown more restraint last night instead of practically throwing herself at Clay? She couldn't blame *that* on the champagne, regardless of its effect.

The truth, clearer now than ever, was that Marisol had wanted him, needed his lovemaking last night. Lovemaking, in her opinion, was the ultimate expression of love, and she would only indulge in that intimacy with the man she planned to marry. If she admitted this to Clay, it would blow any chance of a relationship with him beyond his protection.

Marisol stepped inside the shower stall. She soaped herself vigorously, then rinsed in the hot water, willing it to cleanse her feelings of regret.

By the time she emerged from the bathroom, she had changed into a red sundress. Wearing vivid colors always lifted her spirits, and after thinking about it in the shower, she decided not to let his blunt words hurt her. She would reach out to Clay and encourage him to open up to her. Only then would she understand what drove him to push her away whenever a glimmer of tenderness threatened the rigid emotional control he exercised.

She stepped out of the bathroom. "I'm ready. Let's go," she said, wearing a smile made up of false self-confidence.

Clay followed her lead, carrying their overnight bags out of the hotel. Marisol noticed that he seemed deeply preoccupied with his thoughts as he drove in silence. Stopping briefly at a hardware store, he purchased a double bolt lock for Marisol's front door and special locks for her sliding-glass doors.

They went to Clay's condominium first to pick up his toolbox, then on to Marisol's. When he reached her door, Clay placed a restraining arm across her chest, barring her entrance. "Somebody picked the lock," he said in a low tone. "I'm going in first."

He reached inside his jacket for his semi-automatic pistol. With the tip of the gun, he pushed open the door and cased both sides. He slid inside carefully and braced his legs wide apart, aiming his gun straight ahead. Clay motioned toward the front door with his chin for Marisol to stay put. She stopped in midstride and waited at the front door as he searched her apartment.

Clay bolted from the bedroom and came to Marisol's side. "Follow me, but don't touch anything."

Together, they scanned Marisol's bedroom. Her floral comforter was on the floor, the eyelet-trimmed sheets shredded on her mattress. In the center of the rumpled bed was a broken Barbie doll, eerily dressed in a torn, white linen dress, identical to Marisol's wedding dress. The doll's blond hair had been chopped into a short spiky hairdo.

Marisol stared in wide-eyed shock at the miniature replica of herself. She covered her mouth with shaky hands. "He was in my bedroom. *Dios mío,* I feel so violated!" Rising panic slowed her steps as she walked toward her bed, shock and pain reverberating deep inside her.

"Don't touch anything," Clay commanded. "Come on. I have to go home for my evidence kit. I'll call for a backup when we get there." He grasped her hand and practically dragged her outside.

When they returned to her apartment, Marisol's stomach was churning with fear. She forced herself to make coffee so she wouldn't interrupt Clay while he and another cop worked the apartment for clues. He prepared a crime sketch and dusted for fingerprints, while Detective Gomez completed a detailed report of the room and its contents.

After dismissing Detective Gomez, Clay joined Marisol in the kitchen. "Has anyone visited you lately?"

"Only Luz and Trini have been here lately."

"I'll have to check their fingerprints against what I picked up, so I can isolate the stalker's prints."

"What else did you find?" Preparing herself for the

worst, Marisol tried to keep her hands steady as she set out two steaming mugs of coffee.

"Another note," he bit out, grimly reaching for the mug.

Marisol took a deep breath. "Let me see it."

"No. It's in a plastic bag. I labeled all the items on your bed in plastic bags for investigation."

The soft hairs at the back of her neck prickled her skin ominously. "What was the message this time?"

Marisol watched Clay's handsome face contort with contempt. "It said that you're a slut for marrying me, and the only way you can escape being broken like the doll is to get out of Miami."

"That's bizarre. Now he wants me to leave Miami?" She chewed on her lower lip. "Was anything else on my bed besides the Barbie doll and the note?"

Clay hesitated. "Yes—a Polaroid of you and me arriving at the hotel last night. There was an X drawn over my face in what looks like red lipstick."

She shuddered as horror mingled with outrage at this latest revelation. "I'm fed up with this invasion of my life."

"I won't stop until I catch this bastard."

"Isn't there a law against stalking in Florida?" she asked.

"Just stalking someone is considered a first-degree misdemeanor, punishable by a one thousand dollar fine and/or prison time. Aggravated stalking with the intent to harm, when the victim fears for her physical safety, is a third-degree felony."

"Does that mean jail?"

"Maximum sentence is five years in prison and/or a five thousand dollar fine," he replied. "Before the bill was passed, the only protection was a restraining order, and when that expired, the stalker usually started up again on his victim."

"Why me?"

Clay shrugged. "There's usually a pattern with the stalkers. They victimize somebody they find unattainable and blame them for their failure in relationships or just life in general. I wish I could tell you this will be over soon, but I can't, at least not yet." He reached over to pat her shoulder. "Check your whole apartment thoroughly for anything missing. Concentrate on the bedroom area."

Marisol started systematically going through her apartment. "Clay," she called from the bedroom. "He stole my photo albums and some of my panties and bras!"

An angry tic pulsed in Clay's hard jaw. His manner was brusque and efficient as he focused solely on the crime. Calling downstairs, he questioned Alan about who had recently entered the building. Next, he installed the double bolt security lock on her front door.

"There," he grunted when he was finished. "Let's go."

"Where are we going?" she asked.

Marisol dug in her heels when they reached an apartment door. "Stop ignoring me," she ordered, irritated that he hadn't answered her question.

"You'll stay here in my apartment until I take this evidence into headquarters," he said, opening the door.

"Oh, no, you don't! I'm going with you," she stated.

His mouth formed an intractable line. "No." He took her hand and gently, but firmly dragged her inside.

"Why not?" she asked, yanking her hand out of his grip.

"You'll get in the way."

"Don't talk to me that way. Who made you *el jefe?*" she huffed, annoyed by his sudden change of mood. His attitude no longer seemed protective, but abrupt, and his stern expression showed he meant business. When he remained silent, she said, "I'm the one being stalked. And I don't feel like staying here alone, Blackthorne!"

"Quit arguing." He leaned down to face her squarely, nose to nose. "Stay put till I get back. You'll be safer here." He handed her a small object that looked like a remote control. "This is a panic button connected to the alarm. If you hear anything strange, press this button and the police will come immediately." He kissed the tip of her nose, then turned his broad back and strode out of the apartment.

"Pigheaded tyrant!" Marisol kicked his black leather couch. She resented being left behind at such a crucial time. She wanted to go down to the precinct with him. She tried to calm down while she considered what to do next. Circling the living room, she was surprised to note that it didn't look the least bit lived in. There were no homey touches, no plants, knickknacks or curtains.

Marisol entered his bedroom. On his dresser were two photographs. One, a wedding picture of a smiling couple. The man looked very much like Clay, tall, broad-shouldered, and dark complexioned, but huskier than Clay. The petite woman had dark brown hair and smiling eyes, in a face made charming with deep dimples. They had to be Clay's parents.

Marisol turned her attention to the other photograph. She recognized Clay, at least twenty years younger, with his arm around Jimmy, who was just a little boy in the picture. Her heart warmed at their expressions of brotherhood and strong, mutual love.

A surge of emotion welled up inside her as she suddenly missed her family in Caracas. Marisol sighed deeply and wiped away the moistness gathering in her eyes. There was no use in giving in to homesickness now. That would only serve to weaken her resolve to make it on her own.

Resuming her tour of Clay's apartment, she peeked into his closet. His clothes were hung up, but not in a very orderly fashion. He definitely needed a woman's touch in his apartment. She was intrigued to find a black guitar propped in the corner of the closet. His playing the guitar added another fascinating layer to his personality.

Marisol headed toward the bathroom to explore further. She lifted a bottle of cologne from the counter, uncapped it, and inhaled deeply, remembering his delicious evergreen scent. She closed her eyes and thought of Clay. It couldn't have been just last night that he'd kissed her so passionately. Now he was acting like a general, barking out orders and expecting his commands to be instantly obeyed. He was going to be a bigger challenge than she had anticipated.

A confident smile tugged at the corners of Marisol's mouth. She had faith in her ability to bring him around to her way of thinking. After all, she had been handling an autocrat like Marcos all these years. Many times she had been a terrible pest, resenting the fact that her parents had given him the purse strings to her independence, but Marcos had usually been indulgent as he strove to be fair.

Back in the living room, Marisol began to feel trapped by the stark white walls. She had to get out of there or she'd go nuts. She would go down to the precinct and find out what Clay had learned. Taking one last look around, she placed the panic button in her purse and left Clay's claustrophobic apartment. She passed Alan on her way out and assured him that she was going to meet Clay at the station.

As soon as Marisol got into her car, she opened her sun roof and let the warmth seep into her skin. She suddenly realized that she wasn't sure which police station Clay worked out of. But it was too late to return to the apartment now. Turning out of the parking lot, she drove until she spotted the Rickenbacker Causeway, and began heading toward Key Biscayne. The surrounding ocean was a balm to her nerves. She turned up the volume of the radio and sang with Albita to liven up her mood.

Miles of blue ocean surrounded her on either side. Marisol envied the people basking in the sunshine on their colorful sailboats, oblivious to worries. She watched several small children playing along the shoreline. When would she be able to watch a mother with her baby and not experience a small twinge of envy? she wondered. Marisol knew the answer: once she had a child of her own.

By the time she returned to the apartment, an hour had passed. She ran from the car into the building, worried that Clay would be angry if she wasn't there when he returned.

When she arrived at his apartment, Clay stood in front of the door, his expression foreboding. A shiver ran through Marisol, knowing that her absence had set him off.

"Do you have any idea how worried I was when I got back and didn't find you here?" he demanded in a barely restrained voice.

Marisol watched in mute fascination as a thick vein throbbed in his neck while he fought to regain composure.

"Come inside," he finally said, opening the door for her.

She gave him a small, apologetic smile. "I'm sorry I worried you. I was feeling claustrophobic cooped up in here. I told Alan I was going to meet you at the precinct, but when I got in the car I wasn't sure which station you work out of, so my car automatically led me to the beach instead."

Clay grabbed Marisol's shoulders and curled one hand around her nape as he kissed her hard. "Don't ever do that again."

Her knees almost buckled at the intensity of his kiss. After steadying herself, she shrugged out of his grip.

"This isn't a game, Marisol," he ground out. "I told you to stay put and I meant it. Your life is in danger."

"I was going insane locked up in here. I took your panic button with me into the parking lot. It's here in my purse." She patted her shoulder bag. When his expression didn't soften, she added, "It's broad daylight. I wasn't planning to get out of the car. I was just going for a short drive."

Disgusted, he shook his head and spoke in a low, too-controlled tone. He grasped her shoulders. "Do you know the range of a single slug? A rifle bullet can reach a target over a mile away. The stalker could try anything. Don't forget that for a minute."

"I didn't even consider he might try to shoot me! I meant to be back before you returned."

"You should have never left. I can't protect you unless you obey my orders implicitly." He released her shoulders and took a deep, ragged breath. "You're the only person I know who can bring me this close to losing my cool. In case you haven't forgotten, I'm your bodyguard *and* we're married." His hard countenance held no promise of softening. "I'm setting a few ground rules."

Defiance welled up inside of her. "What ground rules?" she demanded, stiffening before his towering form.

"Rule number one: you don't go anywhere without clearing it with me first. Rule number two: when I give you an order concerning your safety, you follow it. Otherwise, I'm outta here. You can find someone else to guard you."

Clay's hard stare convinced her that he was serious. She was sick to death of taking orders from men. First Marcos, now Clay. She hated having to agree with his rules, but she needed Clay more than ever—and not only as her bodyguard.

"As far as I'm concerned you can eat your ground rules," she said with more bravado than she felt.

Not backing down an inch, his tough gaze held hers. "Do you want someone else to take over this case, Marisol?"

"No." He hadn't called her Sunshine or *nena,* a sure sign that he was serious about his wretched ground rules.

"Then?"

"OK, I'll follow your damn rules, but only until this case is solved." She narrowed her eyes at him. "Now, do I have permission to go to the bathroom, sir?"

"Be my guest," he replied, making a sweeping motion to the bathroom door. His palm itched to smack her impudent little behind as she strutted by.

Once inside the bathroom, Marisol scowled at her image in the mirror. In the privacy of the bathroom, she lamented her reaction to Clay's justified anger. Why was she acting this way? He was right, of course; she had been reckless to go for a drive alone. She decided to apologize and smooth things over.

She entered Clay's bedroom where he sat on the edge of his bed, organizing a black leather satchel. "What are you doing?" she asked, sitting beside him.

"Restocking my evidence collection kit," he replied without looking up.

Marisol could see he was still angry with her. She touched his arm hesitantly, ready to make amends. When he turned to her, she gave him a contrite smile. "Clay, I acted impulsively. I should never have left and caused you to worry about me. It's just that I'm not used to checking in with anybody. I hate having to do that. I'm sorry."

Clay's intense gaze rested on Marisol's mouth for what seemed an eternity. "Apology accepted," he said finally and turned his attention back to his bag.

Marisol's hopes sank when he didn't kiss her. His eyes had practically devoured her mouth, yet he had pulled back, his features controlled. She shifted her weight abruptly on the bed. "What are we doing today?"

"I have a lot of studying to catch up with, but we'll go out to dinner tonight. Where do you go on the weekends?"

"That depends. If I'm in a casual mood, I head to Scotty's in the Grove. They have the freshest seafood and the atmosphere is pretty casual. Some people dock their boats at the restaurant and dine on the outside veranda."

"Do your friends hang out there?" he asked.

"Yes, some of them. Why?"

Clay changed the roll of film in his camera. "Then that's where we're going. We'll leave at seven."

"I need to call Trini and check on the salon. They

were going to do makeovers this afternoon for a spread in *Ocean Drive Magazine*."

"Use the phone in the kitchen," he said.

The kitchen was a delightful surprise, the only room in the apartment that wasn't impersonal. Sunlight streamed in over a row of fresh herbs in terra-cotta pots that lined the windowsill. At the end of the kitchen counter, a round basket brimmed with an assortment of plump peaches, plums, and ripe nectarines.

Marisol opened the refrigerator. A gallon of milk, a pint of orange juice, green grapes, a wedge of provolone cheese and a loaf of pumpernickel bread were on the shelves. Opening a drawer, she saw several raw vegetables, including some she didn't recognize.

Marisol made cheese sandwiches on pumpernickel bread with a touch of dijon mustard and decorated each plate with a dill pickle spear. After rinsing the grapes, she placed them in a bowl. When she finished making lunch, she called Trini.

"I'm so glad you finally called," Trini said.

"Why?"

"You got a phone call this morning, and I've been trying to reach you all day. Gustavo wants to see you!"

Suddenly, Marisol realized that seeing Gustavo leave the restaurant last night might not have been such a coincidence. "What exactly did he say?"

"He wanted to know how to get in touch with you, but I told him you were married now. I didn't give him your new, unlisted phone number," Trini said.

"Thank God you didn't. Where was he calling from?"

"He didn't say."

"Did he leave a number where I can reach him?"

"No. He just said that he needed to see you."

Marisol groaned. "Is everything else going all right?"

"Yes, Maritza and Kyla have been really busy with the makeovers."

"Good. Remember to shut everything off when you lock up."

"Sure thing. How's your husband?" Trini asked.

Marisol smiled. "He's wonderful."

"Aren't you going to take some time off for a honeymoon?"

"Eventually, but not now. Tonight we're having dinner at Scotty's. Thanks for taking charge of the salon. I'll see you Monday," she said, hanging up.

"Who didn't leave his number for you to reach?" Clay asked, startling Marisol. She hadn't heard him walk in during her conversation with Trini.

"Gustavo," she answered. "He wants to see me."

"He could be the person who's been harassing you."

"No. Gustavo is convinced that he has a charming personality. If he was sending me gifts and flowers, he'd want to take all the credit for it."

"What does he do for a living?" Clay asked abruptly.

"He's an actor and a model. He's been doing a lot of commercials lately."

Clay snorted. "How did you get mixed up with him in the first place?"

"You wouldn't understand. Anyway, it's over."

"Not exactly. He wants to make contact with you again," Clay reminded her. "It could be he's enjoying this cat and mouse game. A jilted lover can become obsessed and do strange things. Gustavo could have a split personality."

"Naaah," Marisol replied. "Just because he makes his living as an actor doesn't qualify him as a split personality."

"Where does he live?" Clay asked.

"Last I heard he was living here in South Beach," Marisol answered. "I'm sure he's not the stalker. Besides, the voice over the telephone wasn't his."

"There are ways to disguise your voice," Clay pointed out. "Why did you break off your engagement with him?"

Marisol shrugged. "What I initially thought was love was really infatuation. I didn't want to believe what Marcos said about him because I figured my brother just wanted me back home so he could control my life again. Gustavo was a suave gold-digger with a history of romancing wealthy women. And since my family is financially prominent in Venezuela, he was very interested in me and especially my inheritance from *Abuelito*."

Clay's brows furrowed. "How did he know about your inheritance?"

"I told him. We had talked about investing the money in a state-of-the-art beauty salon. I remember telling him that I would have to use two hundred thousand dollars to open the type of beauty salon I would be proud of. He offered to handle the business matters while I tended to the technical side of running the salon."

"What made you change your opinion about him?"

"A wealthy widow, old enough to be Gustavo's mother, paid me a visit at the salon. She was in tears and blamed me for taking her Gustavo away from her. He had used up her money with his wild spending habits. After I confronted Gustavo, he didn't deny that the woman had been his lover. He said he found older women desirable," Marisol said. "When Marcos showed me evidence that Gustavo had been lying all along about working for an American corporation based in Caracas, I finally believed him. So I broke off the engagement."

"Gustavo could be the stalker," Clay said scornfully.

"I doubt it."

"We'll soon find out." Clay eyed the sandwiches. "Looks good. Let's eat."

"Do you want a beer?" Marisol asked.

"No, I have too much studying to catch up on." Clay winked at her and consumed two sandwiches. After they finished eating lunch, he returned to his studies. Marisol watched him, but his concentration was so deep that he didn't seem to notice her observing him.

Unwittingly, her thoughts were jarred by the image of Gustavo. She couldn't imagine why he would want to talk to her now unless he had somehow heard about Clay. The last time she had seen Gustavo, she'd made it perfectly clear that she never wanted to see him again.

Marisol returned her attention to Clay. He was so different from Gustavo. Clay was exactly as his name implied, as solid as the earth. He was intense and straightforward, and always in charge. He had shed some of that control when he had kissed her last night. His thoughtfulness in providing the hotel suite had been endearing. She could only hope that he would grow to trust her and dispel the strict discipline he kept on his emotions.

At five o'clock, Marisol showered and changed into the same outfit she'd worn the previous night to the hotel. Clay showered after her.

When he was ready, she said, "I'm a little over-dressed for Scotty's. Let's stop at my apartment so I can change clothes."

"OK. But hurry up. I'm hungry."

At her apartment, Marisol quickly changed into a pair of snug black capris, topped by a white French-cut T-shirt.

"Ready?" Clay asked.

"Almost," she said, sliding her small feet into black high-heeled mules. "Wait a minute. I forgot to put on some lipstick."

Clay's dark eyes leisurely appraised her with a look that melted her bones into warm wax. "I prefer you unmade-up. You're more kissable that way." He held her face in his hands and ran his thumb across her lips. "Your bare mouth is such a turn-on."

He tasted her lips, first sucking her full bottom lip into his mouth and then following with her curved upper lip. He kissed the sides of her mouth, then re-captured her lips. He leaned his head back to look at her. "Yes, I'd say you taste much better without lipstick."

Holding Marisol by the nape of her neck with his lean fingers, Clay slid his tongue intimately inside her mouth and kissed her soundly to prove his point. He slid his other hand down her spine and held her pressed against his swelling desire. Marisol's reaction was instantaneous. Hot, wet lust coursed through her as she clung to his shoulders. She moaned when he released her and kissed the bridge of her nose.

"Let's leave," he whispered hoarsely, tearing his gaze away from the ripe swell of her breasts beneath the snug T-shirt. "Otherwise I won't be responsible for what comes next." Clay straightened away from her. "We'll never leave if we get started. There's a purpose for going to Scotty's tonight. If you're being followed, the stalker will see us together," he said, suddenly all business.

"All right," she agreed with a little pout.

He watched her strut ahead of him, thinking how cute her backside looked in those capri pants. "Later," he promised, thinking, *we have all evening.*

Scotty's was packed as usual. They stood at the outdoor straw-covered bar where Marisol sipped a piña colada while Clay drank a draft beer. Several people approached Marisol and greeted her as she introduced them to her new husband. Their table was soon ready and a tanned waitress in a floral sarong seated them next to the ocean.

"I recommend the mahimahi," Marisol said, studying the menu. "They grill it to perfection and serve it with a fresh mango-lime chutney on the side."

Clay closed his menu. "Sounds great to me."

"I think I'll have the grilled salmon in the ginger and cilantro glaze. That way we can share." She closed the menu and looked around her. "This is the only restaurant I know of where dogs can wander in without being thrown out." Marisol followed Clay's surprised look to a frisky labrador retriever that was just getting off a docked sailboat with its owner.

When the friendly white lab reached their table, Clay said, "It looks like he's a regular here." He reached over to pet it. "One of these days I'll buy a house with a backyard large enough for two dogs."

"Did you have a dog when you were growing up?"

"No, but I wish Jimmy did. I'd buy him a puppy if they allowed it where he lives."

"I saw the picture of the two of you on your dresser. Your relationship with Jimmy is really special."

Clay smiled warmly. *"He's* special."

When they finished dinner and were waiting for key lime pie and coffee, Clay's beeper sounded.

"I have to make a phone call." He ambled toward the pay telephone on the outside wall of the restaurant and dialed the precinct. From his vantage point, he could see Marisol dimly. Halfway through the conversation he saw someone dressed in black approach Marisol and a brief struggle between them ensued. Clay roared into the receiver, "Send a backup unit to Scotty's in the Grove! NOW!"

Clay dropped the telephone and took off on a dead run toward the dock, his only thought to rescue Marisol. His heart hammered savagely against his heaving chest as he bolted toward her.

Seven

Clay raced toward Marisol. The man grabbed her about the waist and slung her, kicking and screaming, over his broad shoulder. He carried her to a waiting speedboat and jumped into the boat. After dumping Marisol on the floor, he maneuvered the boat from the dock.

Clay heard Marisol scream, "BLACKTHORNE!" He swore a round of curses as fierce rage scorched his gut. As Clay ran toward the dock, the kidnapper's speedboat erupted into the black, moonless night. Clay jumped into the closest speedboat and tried frantically to start it. When that didn't work, he leaped into a newer, Cigarette Warrior speedboat. He punched the electronic controls and the engine started. Pure adrenaline jolted through his body when he pushed up the throttle and floored the engine.

Clay's damp shirt stretched across his back, plastered against his straining muscles, and his pistol dug into his shin. Police work was dangerous and unpredictable, but he had always handled it impassively, for his own survival. Now this was different—Marisol's safety was at stake, not his, and his concern for her had nothing to do with his promise to Marcos.

Clay felt like tearing the kidnapper apart with his

bare hands when he thought about how roughly the man had thrown Marisol's petite body over his shoulder. He made himself breathe deeply and slowly, consciously reining in his fury. Excessive anger would only weaken his concentration and hamper his coordination.

Hot on their trail, Clay turned on the boat lights, his warrior instincts screaming for revenge.

Gustavo slowed down and stopped the boat when they were way out at sea, far away from other boats. He slid his hands down the sides of Marisol's body. "Does it hurt anywhere?" he asked with an insolent grin.

"Get your hands off me, you idiot!" Marisol cried.

"I was just checking for damage."

"Touch me again and I'll kick you where it counts."

"Is that any way to talk to your lover?"

"Shut up!" She backed away from him on the small boat. "Why did you kidnap me?"

"Aren't you happy that I rescued you from your boring date?"

"Clay is my husband."

"So, it's true. I can't believe you actually married that guy on the rebound."

"You jackass! I married Clay because I'm in love with him, much more than I ever loved you. How did you know I'd be here? Did you follow me?"

Gustavo chucked her under the chin. "I didn't have to follow you. Trini told me you'd be having dinner at Scotty's tonight."

Marisol knocked his offending hand away from her chin. "Trini has a big mouth."

Gustavo's eyes twinkled. "Come here, *corazón*. Give me a little kiss."

"I'd rather kiss garbage! Why have you been following me and torturing me with your sick, twisted pranks?"

He stared at her. "What are you babbling about?"

"Don't act innocent! I saw you leaving La Palma last night."

He chuckled and reached over to muss the top of her head. *"Sí, I was at La Palma, y por qué no?"*

"I already warned you not to touch me," she said, her body quaking with fury. "Explain why you were at the same restaurant last night."

Gustavo shrugged his broad shoulders. "I like Italian food. I don't need to follow you for that."

"I know you're the stalker. Why have you been terrorizing me with your perverted games?"

"What stalker? What perverted games?" he demanded, his expression a mixture of affront and bewilderment.

Baffled by his dumbfounded reaction, Marisol reminded herself that Gustavo was a competent actor. "Are you telling me that you haven't been sending me flowers and weird gifts?"

"That would be impossible—I only arrived in Miami last week. I've been shooting some commercials on location in Cancún for the past two weeks."

She still didn't believe him. "If you're not the stalker, then why did you kidnap me from the restaurant?"

"For the thrill of it. What happened to your sense of adventure? You used to love that sort of thing," he said. "It must be your new husband's influence on you."

"Leave Clay out of this!" she snapped, fed up with Gustavo's conceited sarcasm.

"OK, OK. Calm down." Gustavo's voice became melodic. "I still love you, *tesoro*. I didn't believe Trini when she said you were married. I figured you probably wouldn't agree to see me, so I had to use some inventive persuasion." He winked at her suggestively. "Now we can talk in private."

"You're insane!"

Gustavo eyes took on a wounded, puppy-dog look. The man was capable of summoning up emotion with mercurial speed. "Not insane, *mi linda,* just in love. Deeply in love with you."

She covered her ears. "I don't want to hear any more lies," she yelled over the sudden noise of another engine. "Take me back now!"

"Not until you listen to me," Gustavo shouted back. "I can't let you go back until you admit you still love me." He looked over his shoulder toward the noise and bright lights suddenly behind them. "It looks like your husband wants to play hero." Gustavo's mouth twisted bitterly as he started the engine and accelerated.

"Clay is a police detective and he's armed. Stop or he'll shoot you."

Gustavo's eyes widened. "Why didn't you warn me before? I don't want any trouble with the police," he said, reluctantly slowing the engine to a stop.

Clay swerved sharply to the right to avoid ramming headfirst into Gustavo's boat. He slowed the engine and returned to Gustavo's boat. With his pistol pointing directly at Gustavo, he shouted, "FREEZE, POLICE!"

Gustavo threw up his hands in mock surrender and grinned broadly. "Don't shoot me. It was just a little prank."

Holding the Beretta at eye level with Gustavo, Clay reached over and helped Marisol board his boat. His eyes swept over her as he checked for injuries. "Did he hurt you?"

Marisol shook her head. "I'm not hurt, just furious at him."

"Can you man the steering wheel?" he asked Marisol tersely.

She looked at the controls in dismay. "I wish I knew how."

Clay motioned with his gun toward Gustavo. "Get in," he bellowed. "Keep your hands up."

Gustavo scrambled aboard Clay's boat with his hands above his head. "Take us back to the dock. No sudden moves or you'll be sorry," Clay warned.

At first, Gustavo belligerently followed Clay's instructions. He showed his usual bravado by turning to Marisol with a slick smile and putting his hands up coolly. In a seductive whisper, he said, *"Corazón,* please. Tell him I'm not the stalker." When Marisol ignored him, Gustavo changed his tune and pleaded, "Don't let him arrest me." He put his hands together in supplication. *"Por favor,* I'm innocent!"

"Shut up and drive," Clay snarled, pointing his gun at him.

"But what about my boat?" Gustavo asked.

"The police will get it later. Drive!" Clay thundered.

Gustavo brought them swiftly back to shore. A backup unit of policemen was waiting on the restaurant dock where a cluster of restaurant patrons surrounded a police car. They gawked as Clay arrested Gustavo, read him his rights, and handcuffed him. Considerably subdued, Gustavo rode in the back of the patrol car while Marisol and Clay followed closely behind in Clay's car.

"I can't believe Gustavo kidnapped me," Marisol said, shaking her head.

"I thought he might try to make a move on you," Clay said in disgust. "What did he say to you in the boat?"

"A bunch of drivel about still being in love with me. Then when I confronted him about the sick games he's been playing with me, he denied being the stalker."

"Do you believe him?" Clay asked, glancing at her.

"I'm not sure now. He seemed to know nothing about the flowers and gifts. But then, he is a convincing liar."

"How did he defend himself?"

"He said he couldn't have been the one harassing me since he just arrived from Cancún last week after filming commercials."

"I can easily check that out." Clay's eyes narrowed as he assessed her. "Did he get rough with you?"

Marisol shook her head. "No. But he's convinced that we should get back together."

Clay snorted. "Fat chance."

"Fat chance is right! I can't believe his gall tonight. He's probably thrilled he'll get free publicity from all this. I don't know what to make of him anymore."

"I can only hold him for seventy-two hours. By then I should be able to prove he's the one who's been stalking you."

By the time they arrived at the police station, Gustavo was struggling with the police officers, demanding to call his lawyer and threatening to sue Clay. When he was warned that he'd be charged with resisting arrest, Gustavo shut up momentarily. After the necessary paperwork, he was booked on attempted kidnapping charges and suspicion of aggravated stalking. He complained loudly about being held without bail when he was taken to a waiting cell.

* * *

Marisol was still shaken over the evening's disastrous events when they returned late that night to Clay's apartment.

"What a horrible evening!" She flung her shoulder bag on the couch and kicked off her high-heeled mules.

Clay sat down next to her and placed his arm around her shoulders, tucking her beside him. "Now that we've identified him, it makes the investigation a lot easier if he is the stalker."

"What if he isn't?" she asked anxiously.

Clay's grim expression was resolute. "Then I'll track down whoever it is."

"I hope so. I never want to go through an ordeal like that again." She leaned her head against his arm and examined the austere living room. There were two black leather couches, a glass coffee table with two matching end tables, a chrome floor lamp, and a copy of the morning's newspaper. "How long have you lived here?" she asked suddenly.

"Not very long. Why?"

"Where are your personal belongings? You know, paintings, knickknacks."

Clay chuckled mirthlessly. "I don't own any knickknacks. The rest of my things are still sitting in boxes. I haven't had a chance to get organized and unpacked. I've been working long hours and studying for the bar."

She was sure her predicament was the reason he hadn't been able to make his apartment into a home. "I guess my problems haven't helped either."

"It's my job," he said matter-of-factly.

"Still, I'd like to help. I can unpack for you."

"No," he said brusquely, then softened it by adding,

"I have some things to clear out first. Thanks for offering, but I'm the only one who can do it."

Clay propped his legs on the coffee table and reached down to place Marisol's feet on his lap. With skilled hands, he massaged the arch of her dainty feet and moved on to her brightly painted toes. "Cute toes," he observed.

"You're spoiling me," she said, sighing happily. "The greatest treat in the world is a good massage."

"Then we'll do this right." Clay stood and led Marisol from the sofa into the bedroom, where he folded down the comforter. "Wait for me here." He went into the bathroom and returned with a towel and a small bottle of oil. "Take off your clothes," he said, handing her the towel, "and wrap yourself in this."

Her eyes widened at his brazen request. "I am *not* going to strip down bare for a massage. I'd rather keep my clothes on."

Clay's mouth quirked up into a slow, sexy smile. "A good massage can only be done on bare skin. You can drape the towel over your hips."

"Gee, that's comforting," she quipped, in an attempt to hide her sudden shyness. A warm flush infused her body from the tip of her head to the tips of her toes just imagining herself lying before him with only a towel covering her bottom. Marisol ached to feel his strong hands soothing and gentling her body.

Without another word, she took the towel and went to his walk-in closet. She stood still and inhaled deeply, enjoying the masculine scent of leather and cedar. She undressed to her panties and hung her clothes next to Clay's, shivering deliciously as she envisioned the massage to come. Clad only in her bikini panties, Marisol wrapped the towel around her torso, covering the essentials. She approached the bed and stood beside Clay, her knees almost buckling with anticipation.

"Lie on your belly." His low voice stirred her senses, making her breath catch in her throat.

Making sure the towel was securely wrapped around her, Marisol stretched facedown on his bed and leaned her cheek against her folded arms.

"Leave your hands at your sides so your back can be fully relaxed," he coaxed.

Marisol's heart skipped a beat when she heard Clay uncap the oil and pour a little into his palms. Glancing over her shoulder, she watched his dark hands rub together. A little moan escaped her when his warm hands made contact with her sensitized skin. Normally, a massage relaxed her to a state of blissful limpness. But not tonight. Every nerve in her body was alert, on edge, jumping with giddy anticipation.

"Relax," he said, his deep voice sending a ripple of excitement through her. Clay massaged her shoulders in slow, rotating circles. His thumbs pressed and released the soft flesh of her nape rhythmically; then his hands swept down each arm alternately with firm but gentle strokes.

Marisol's breath quickened when Clay loosened the towel and lowered it to her waist, but she couldn't bring herself to object when his hands made contact with her bare back. He placed his fingers on either side of her spine, massaging her with long, sweeping movements. When his large hands fanned outward from her spine, his fingertips grazing the sides of her breasts, hot, wet desire gushed straight to her feminine core.

He moved to the small of her back, and his thumbs

brushed just under the edge of the towel covering her buttocks. When she thought she'd go insane with wondering how far the massage would go, he switched his attention to her feet. After applying more oil to his hands, he massaged her feet expertly, giving each toe individual attention before moving up to her calves in smooth, firm movements. Turning his attention to her lower thighs, he applied a bit more pressure, causing her to squirm.

"Was that too hard?" he asked, his warm breath inches from her ear.

"No, it's perfect," she barely managed, biting the sheets to prevent from moaning.

When Clay's strong hands reached the tops of her thighs, he placed one arm around Marisol's waist, lifting her enough to dislodge the towel. Any objection died in her throat when he removed the towel. Marisol's skin tingled and throbbed and she wondered if the rest of her body was as flushed pink as her face felt. Breathlessly, she awaited the return of his touch as he poured more oil onto his hands.

"That smells good," she murmured, her voice sounding hoarse. "What is it?"

"Grapeseed oil."

"Really?" She shifted her body so she could look at him.

Clay's hand rested on the back of her upper thigh, sending another pulsating jolt to the juncture of her thighs. "Shh," he crooned, "You're supposed to be quiet and let the tension flow from your body."

He stroked her back maddeningly from her shoulders, down her indented spine, to just above the edge of her sheer black panties. Every nerve ending in her skin palpitated with excitement. Clay returned to her upper thighs and massaged them firmly. "Such baby-soft skin," he murmured huskily.

"*Ay*, Blackthorne, that feels sooo good," she whimpered, biting her lower lip until she thought she would draw blood. Marisol almost leaped off the bed when Clay slipped his warm, rough-textured hands under the silky legs of her panties and firmly kneaded her bottom. Helplessly, her spine arched with the agony of sweet anticipation.

Completing the task to his satisfaction and her undoing, he coaxed Marisol over onto her back.

When her hungry gaze met his, Clay's eyes were shimmering black pools of erotic invitation. She quivered as he stroked her pale breasts with lean brown fingers. Her aching nipples tightened to pebble-hardness at his touch.

"*Nena,* I was so frantic tonight when Gustavo kidnapped you." His gruff whisper held evidence of the overwhelming distress he'd experienced. "I need to make love to you," he said, his voice raw with arousal. He bent his head toward her bosom, held in his oil-slick hands, and deposited soft kisses to the plump perimeter of her breasts, then suckled her tender nipples—his tongue like velvet against the aching tips.

Marisol looked at Clay, his handsome face flushed with stark desire. "I want you," she whispered. "I *need* you. Now!"

Clay reached into the nightstand drawer and withdrew a small package of condoms. He turned out the light and stripped off his clothes to slip on the condom. Turning toward her, he grasped her panties and slid them down her hips, then tossed them aside.

"God, you're beautiful," he said, kneeling between her widespread thighs. He rained kisses onto her quivering belly, dipping his hot tongue into her navel and moving lower. Her body convulsed in tiny spasms when she felt his warm breath tickling her sensitive flesh. Marisol gasped at the sweet insanity taking over her as she clutched his thick hair. "Make love to me. Please!"

She felt Clay raise his muscular body to lie on top of her as his thumb reached between her legs and stroked her slick arousal. In sweet agony, she arched upward and dug her nails into his shoulders. "Come inside, *mi amor*," she urged.

Sliding his broad hands beneath her buttocks, he gently squeezed, then lifted her hips and eased himself inside. Her nipples, damp from his kisses, strained against his chest as he repeatedly thrust inside of her. Marisol's nails grazed his back as she bucked beneath him, matching his hammering rhythm. Clay grasped her thighs and lifted them high as he drove hard and deep.

She went wild, whimpering and grasping his tight, muscular hips as her body contracted in a shattering orgasm. He covered her mouth with his and thrust until he reached his climax, the veins in his neck bulging when he gave a primal shout of release.

Clay hugged her tightly. "Was I too rough?" he asked afterward, his voice soft with tenderness.

Fused to his magnificent body, Marisol had never experienced such unspeakable joy. "No, I wanted you that badly, too," she reassured him, blinking back exhilarated tears.

"You're mine, *Nena*," he growled fiercely. "I'm possessive. Even after I arrest the stalker. You're mine."

Silent tears flowed down the sides of Marisol's face, dampening her pillow. She had desperately needed to hear him say those affirming words. Clay rolled to his side and positioned her body spoon fashion with her back resting against his chest. When he kissed the sensitive nape of her neck, she felt him shudder slightly. "To think I almost lost you!" he rasped, his voice raw with emotion.

Marisol was deeply touched that he'd revealed tender feelings for her, especially since he was so guarded with his emotions. She loved Clay so much it hurt, and the intensity of it scared her. From their first meeting, when he had stoically endured her teasing, to the moment when she'd witnessed his devoted love for Jimmy, she had been falling hopelessly in love with him.

She needed time to find out why he didn't consider himself good marriage material, as he'd once warned her. She forced herself to block those thoughts from her mind and heart for now. Tonight she would allow herself the luxury of reveling in a fantasy come true. She snuggled back against his chest and attempted to fall asleep in his powerful arms.

Shaken to the core by the evening's events, Clay lay awake for a long time afterward. That was the closest he'd ever come to saying "I love you" to any woman after Jillian. It was the best he could do. A palpable ache in his heart told him that Marisol had to be his.

Flinching, he suddenly remembered Marcos. It was too late to worry about the consequences his actions would have on their friendship. He only hoped his valued friend would understand.

But that wasn't the only reason for his sleeplessness. Deep in his heart, he knew he'd never be able to give Marisol what she'd be sure to want—a real marriage and children. After his divorce from Jillian, he had made a solemn vow that he'd never remarry again, and he meant to keep it. He'd have to find a way to keep Marisol in his life without staying married or having children.

When Marisol awakened the following morning, she found herself alone in Clay's bed. She wandered out to the living room and watched Clay, dressed in sweats and a T-shirt, practicing T'ai Chi in the sunlight on his balcony. No wonder he seemed to have mastered the technique for calming down and remaining centered most of the time. He moved as if in a trance, bending, twisting, weaving his body in slow graceful movements resembling an exotic dance.

She marveled at how she never tired of admiring his rare masculine beauty. Mesmerized, she watched his movements change from controlled gracefulness to quicksilver fighting techniques. With a series of sharp, explosive kicks and strikes, he snaked across the balcony in rapid-fire movements that created a jarring contrast to the smooth fluidity of T'ai Chi. Marisol wished she could see his bare torso as his muscles bunched and stretched alternately.

She suddenly realized that he'd already seen her twice in the nude, but she'd never seen his unclothed body in the light. When they had made love, it had been in the dark. Now she wondered if he might have done it on purpose, perhaps to hide a scar. Not wanting to interrupt his ritual, Marisol tiptoed back to the bathroom where she showered and changed.

From the bedroom, she could smell the rich aroma of percolating Cuban coffee. When she joined Clay in the kitchen, he was sitting at the counter drinking a cup of *café con leche*. *The Miami Herald* was strewn across the counter as he read with interest.

"Good morning," Marisol said, kissing his unshaven jaw. "Mind if I join you?" She knew he was a private person, and she felt a bit uneasy sharing his space so casually. It had been different when they were sharing her apartment, because they hadn't made love yet. Now, despite their intimacy the previous night, Clay's presence unsettled her, especially in the cozy environment of his kitchen.

"Help yourself to coffee." When he glanced up from reading the paper, the stubble on his lean face combined with his heated gaze gave him a sinfully dangerous aura.

Their eyes locked for a charged moment and Marisol felt her insides melt. With shaky hands, she poured herself a cup of coffee and refilled his mug. "I want to go home," she announced, tearing her gaze from his. "I need to check my answering machine and get fresh clothing to change into." Although Marisol had no appetite, she reached for a ripe peach to fill her empty stomach. "Have you had breakfast already?"

"Yeah. I've already checked in with the precinct for an update on Gustavo."

"How is he?" she inquired, not really anxious to know.

Clay grunted. "He became subdued once he realized he couldn't be released yet, even with a lawyer. I ordered an FBI fingerprint search to find out if he's ever been arrested."

Marisol gulped. "Has he?"

"We'll know by tomorrow morning when I check his fingerprints against the latents I picked up in your apartment."

"Latents?" Marisol repeated quizzically.

"The fingerprints I dusted and transferred onto a special card." Clay turned the newspaper page and continued reading.

Marisol bit into the peach and used her napkin to dab at her lower lip. "I think I'll go to my apartment now."

Clay raised his hand, detaining her from leaving. "We'll go together. After you pack what you need, we'll move it here."

"I need to go to the market today, so I can buy something to prepare for dinner."

"There's no need to. We're invited for dinner at Isabel and Linc's tonight."

"Who are they?"

"Some close friends of mine who own a fruit tree nursery in the Redlands."

Marisol's heart did a little leap of joy. She was flattered that he wanted his friends to meet her. This was the first invitation they would accept as a couple, but she shouldn't make too big a deal out of it. "What time are we going?" she asked, trying to contain the urge to smile broadly.

"We'll leave by six-fifteen. It takes about forty-five minutes to get there."

"What about your studies?"

"I'll study during the day. I haven't seen Linc and Isabel for months. Tonight we'll be celebrating because they're expecting another baby."

"Do they have other children?"

"Yeah. Suzie, Isabel's daughter from her first marriage, is eight and T.J. is two."

"Someday I plan to have three children," she said, smiling at him.

Clay's mouth twitched. "Three? I wouldn't even want one child at my age."

"What do you mean? You're not too old to have a child," she scoffed.

"Jimmy is all the family I need. Believe me. I have no desire to be a daddy at my age." He grimaced in horror. "Linc is a brave man. It's a good thing we used protection last night because we don't need an unwanted pregnancy."

Marisol's hopeful heart sank at his callous words. She searched his face, hoping for some sign that he hadn't really meant it. For a brief moment she thought she might have seen a flicker of regret in his beautiful eyes, but then it was gone.

Eight

That afternoon, Marisol tried to nap, but Clay's words kept tormenting her. *"It's a good thing we used protection last night because we don't need an unwanted pregnancy."* Every time she relived their conversation, she wanted to cry. The previous night he had been passionate and tender during the most exquisite lovemaking she had ever experienced. He had told her that she belonged to him and she wanted to believe him. But there was one little problem—she yearned for a real marriage and children. Now she was afraid to voice that sentiment.

From the bedroom she could hear Clay talking to Jimmy on the telephone. When he returned, she asked, "How's Jimmy?"

"He's OK. He understood that I couldn't take him out today. I'll make it up to him later."

"Do you think he'll ever fall in love?"

Clay frowned. "Where did that come from? Jimmy doesn't need those type of complications."

"Everybody needs a little romance."

"Maybe, but I didn't miss having it after I split from my ex-wife, Jillian."

"What was she like?" Marisol asked, thrilled that he had finally brought up the subject of his ex.

"I'd rather not talk about her."

"Oh, come on," she coaxed.

Clay's jaw tightened. "She was selfish."

Marisol flinched at his caustic tone. "Was she very beautiful?" She watched his features harden as he regarded her in stubborn silence.

"OK then, don't answer that one. But tell me what happened." If he didn't open up to her, how would she ever understand where he was coming from? "Please," she added.

He let out a ragged breath. "I thought I knew her, but she didn't show her true colors until after we were married. Jillian is a journalistic photographer. Her biggest goal in life is professional success, no matter how many colleagues she tramples to achieve that. She can be mean-spirited and ruthless."

"When did you divorce her?"

Clay's face became shuttered, his eyes stony. "Let's change the subject."

Marisol ignored his vehement tone. "Come on, Blackthorne. It's only fair. I already told you about Gustavo."

"That's different."

Marisol huffed. "I'm not buying that."

"We'll talk later. I need to study."

Marisol allowed him to think he could quell her curiosity, but she'd try to get some answers at the next opportunity. She occupied her time by arranging Clay's closet to make room for her clothes. During the hours he spent reading, Marisol changed the bed sheets and threw in a load of his wash. Clay had so much on his mind between work, studying, and especially protecting her, that Marisol didn't mind doing those domestic chores for him. In fact, she had to admit that a little part of her delighted in them, making her feel truly married and intimate with Clay.

An hour before it was time to leave for dinner, Marisol walked into the dining room and saw Clay sitting at the table, engrossed in his law book. She stole up behind him and nuzzled the thick, coarse hair at the back of his neck. "I'm going to freshen up now before we leave," she said, depositing a soft kiss on his nape.

"OK," he mumbled, not looking up from his book.

So much for romance, she thought. He was so absorbed in his studies that he hadn't even responded to her caress. She was caught off guard when he finally turned and his warm hand slipped beneath the back hem of her shorts and gently squeezed her skin. He retrieved his hand and slid it across the swell of her bottom, then up under her crop top, along her spine until it rested at her nape, his fingers tickling the soft hairs there. "If you hurry, we might have time for a little massage."

Marisol gulped and gripped the edge of the table. Walking on wobbly limbs, she somehow made it to the bathroom where she took an invigorating shower, staying longer than necessary to quell the raging desire he had ignited.

Slightly calmer now, Marisol blow-dried her hair and pondered how to approach the subject of his divorce with Jillian again. She needed to know why he was so turned off to marriage and having babies. She didn't believe for a minute that he felt too old to have a baby. She remembered when he'd said, *"I plan to keep my vow never to remarry."* Jillian must have done something really awful for Clay not to want to remember or talk about the divorce.

After her shower, Marisol changed into a turquoise

sundress and high-heeled sandals. Clay walked into the bathroom while she was styling her hair.

"You shouldn't wear high heels," he murmured, his voice husky with desire.

Marisol whirled around. "I didn't even hear you walk in," she said, amazed at how silently he could move for a man his size. "Why shouldn't I wear high heels?" she asked coyly.

He softly nipped her nape. "You look too sexy in them."

Marisol shivered. The gentle bite on her sensitive skin nearly buckled her knees as she remembered their lovemaking of the previous night. "I wasn't too comfortable either while you were studying. Now it's your turn to suffer." She gave him a naughty grin before turning away.

"Tease," he growled, sucking her earlobe.

Instant gooseflesh formed at Marisol's nape and she felt her toes curl. "If you don't stop, we're going to be late," she faltered, breathing rapidly.

He flashed a lazy grin of pure masculine promise. "OK, but when we return, I plan to savor your pink little earlobes, and a lot more." He sauntered out of the bathroom. Marisol would have let him savor anything right there if he had initiated it. The fact that she'd have to wait until the evening only heightened her arousal. No one had ever made her react so quickly and lose complete control.

The long drive to Isabel and Linc's home provided the perfect opportunity for Marisol to broach the subject of Clay's divorce. "Clay," she began sweetly, "finish telling me about your divorce."

"Why are you so interested?" he asked, sounding mildly annoyed.

"I don't mean to be nosy, but it will help me understand where you're coming from," she said, hoping to encourage him to open up.

Clay regarded her with exaggerated patience. "In the short time I've known you, you haven't been able to graciously take 'no' for an answer."

Marisol squelched the urge to grin. He was right; she never gave up easily. If she wanted to know something she would persist until she got her answers.

"All right, we'll talk about my divorce this one time and then it's a closed subject. Understand?"

Marisol nodded with feigned submission. "I won't bring it up again."

Clay took a deep breath and watched her with solemn eyes. "Jillian aborted our child without my knowledge. When I found out, I divorced her."

Marisol's heart constricted at the anguish on his face. "Why would she do that?"

"She said she didn't want to have a baby because it would interfere with her career. But that wasn't the real reason." His mouth twisted bitterly. "She aborted our baby because she was afraid it might be mentally handicapped like Jimmy. She said she'd be devastated and could never deal with *'a retarded kid like that'*."

Clay clutched the steering wheel and turned to look at her. His face looked like an open wound, and she saw the raw pain transform his features. "Jillian terminated an innocent life for selfish reasons, Marisol. It was my baby, too."

"Oh, God." She felt as if she had been punched in the stomach. "I'm so sorry, Clay. I shouldn't have pried."

Grim-faced, he remained silent for a while before saying, "You couldn't have known."

Her heart went out to him. "I can understand how Jillian might have been worried about her baby being mentally handicapped. But I can't imagine anybody having an abortion in the cold-blooded way you describe. If I were Jillian, I would have been delighted to have your baby," she said truthfully.

He studied her face with fathomless eyes, as black as the midnight ocean. "You wouldn't have worried about Jimmy's problem?"

"Not at all," she said sincerely. "Jimmy is a wonderful person. The possibility of having a disabled child wouldn't have made me consider an abortion. I would love any child of ours," she assured him. "I have enough love in my heart for all types of children."

Clay's hand folded over Marisol's and he held it in a warm, tight grip. "Not everyone is as generous and brave as you are, Sunshine."

"Thank you," she whispered, tears springing to her eyes. Jillian's abortion had destroyed Clay's faith in love, and Marisol felt miserable for him.

Clay slowed his car to a stop at the red light and turned to look at her. "I didn't mean to make you cry. All that's behind me now," he said, kissing the tear that had slipped down her cheek. "I don't miss being married or having children."

"Someday you'll realize you're just fooling yourself, and you'll learn to trust women again."

"Women," he muttered. "Our own mother abandoned Jimmy as soon as she found herself another husband and manipulated him into moving back to Buenos Aires. She couldn't deal with a burden like

Jimmy, and she was afraid that he would ruin her chances of a second marriage. Those were her exact words."

"How cruel!" Now everything was beginning to make sense to her. "So you became Jimmy's guardian. Is that why you postponed law school?"

"Yeah, I became a police officer because it was shift work and allowed me to spend time with *mi hermanito*."

"You must be proud of him. Jimmy's so loving and he's made a productive life for himself working at the grocery store."

"He *has* become pretty independent. Jimmy lived with me after my mom left, but one day when I was working undercover narc, I almost got killed. I realized I wasn't doing him any favors by sheltering him from the outside world, since I might not always be there to protect him. So I found a place for him to live where he could make friends and work nearby. The Haven of Hope has an excellent program, and Jimmy's never been happier. He's so proud of his paycheck every week."

"Do you take care of his living expenses?" she asked.

"I don't need to. Our dad was a lawyer; he left a generous amount for Jimmy's needs in his will. He'll be well provided for until he dies."

After a brief silence, Marisol touched his arm. "Clay, I'm not like Jillian or your mother. You can trust me. I'll stay beside you as long as you want me." She paused. *"If* you still want that," she said, reminding him of his possessive words after their lovemaking.

"I do," he said, squeezing her hand.

Clay turned off Krome Avenue onto a dirt road. When they reached the large circular driveway leading to Linc and Isabel's house, Marisol felt instantly drawn to their fertile land. Hundreds of royal palms and tropical fruit trees surrounded the Mediterranean-style house.

"What a gorgeous place! It belongs in a movie."

"I thought you'd like it. It's quite a change from hectic Miami, isn't it?"

"I'll say!" Nearing the house, Marisol saw a man standing with his arm draped across the shoulders of a woman as they watched two small children at play. Linc was tall and handsome with brown hair and blue eyes and Isabel was lovely with long, straight black hair and expressive dark brown eyes.

"Come inside," Isabel said warmly after they were introduced. Marisol detected a slight Cuban accent. "Linc can check the *lechon* while I make us some drinks. He's had it slow-cooking on the rotisserie."

"It smells great," Clay said. "Did you make my favorite black beans and rice?"

"Of course." Isabel turned to her daughter. "Suzie, let Tío Clay breathe now," she admonished. Although not really related, Suzie called Clay uncle as a term of endearment.

"Stay right where you are, Suzie," he said, winking at her. She had her sturdy little arms wound tightly around Clay's waist, who was holding T.J.

Linc turned to Clay and Marisol. "Let's go onto the patio. You can see the new swimming pool."

Isabel joined them shortly on the patio with a tray of drinks and a basket of crisp tortilla chips with a spicy salsa dip. They settled in for an animated conversation. Marisol liked Isabel immediately. They were close to the same age and even though their lifestyles were very different, Isabel had once run a business on her own and Marisol found that they had much in common.

Marisol looked out at their lush backyard. A pink glow from the setting sun lent a sparkle to the fertile rows of citrus trees. Suzie and T.J. played in the yard with Mango, their pet golden retriever. What a truly idyllic surrounding for raising children!

Later, they went inside the kitchen so Isabel could prepare an avocado salad. While Isabel squeezed lime juice over the avocado chunks and thinly sliced onions, Marisol glanced out of the window and observed Clay and Linc at the barbecue grill. Clay had remained close friends with Linc even after Linc had retired from the police force.

On the drive to their home, Clay had told Marisol how Isabel had led Linc on a merry chase before agreeing to marry him. Clay had admitted that he'd initially thought Isabel was more trouble than she was worth, until he'd gotten to know her. Now he understood why Linc would have been willing to change his lifestyle so drastically for Isabel to agree to marry him.

"The pork's ready, Isabelita," Linc called out. "Is everything else set up?"

"Yes, bring it in."

They enjoyed a feast of succulent roast pork, rice and beans, and fried sweet plantains. Suzie and T.J. had been fed earlier, but Clay allowed T.J. to sit on his lap, munching happily on a piece of Cuban bread. Marisol was amused by Clay's patience with T.J. as the little boy talked gibberish and shared his bread.

Isabel and Marisol cleared the table while Linc showed Clay his new fertilizing equipment. Suzie had taken T.J. with her to her bedroom to play. When they finished rinsing the dishes and stacking them into the dishwasher, Marisol helped Isabel get the children ready for bed.

"How long have you known Clay?" Marisol asked Isabel as she watched her dress T.J. in blue cotton pajamas.

"About three years. You're the first woman he's ever brought for us to meet."

"Really? That's good news," Marisol said, grinning.

Isabel smiled at Marisol. "You're in love with him, aren't you?"

"Is it that obvious?"

Isabel laughed delightedly. "Are you kidding? You two haven't been able to keep your eyes off each other all evening!"

"I haven't noticed him staring at me."

"I have, and from the looks of it, I'd say he's in deep. I never thought I'd see the day he'd fall in love again."

"Why not?" Marisol followed Isabel into Suzie's room.

"Because since I've known him he's been a diehard cynic about love. His vow not to remarry is famous at the police station."

"Did you ever meet his ex-wife, Jillian?" Marisol asked, still curious about her.

"No, but Linc says she was a witch."

"That sounds like Clay's description."

Isabel gave her an incredulous look. "He told you about Jillian?"

"Yes, well I had to pry it out of him. Why do you look so shocked?"

"Because that subject has always been taboo with Clay." Isabel stopped talking when Suzie, freshly showered and in her nightgown, walked into the bedroom. Suzie tucked T.J. next to her in her bed for a bedtime story. After Isabel shared a prayer in Spanish with them, she called Linc to join her in kissing them good night. Marisol was ashamed to feel a small pang of envy mixed in with her admiration of the cozy domestic scene before her. Just then, Clay walked in and kissed both children good night after promising to take them to the beach one day soon.

They retired to the living room and Isabel served *flan de coco* with strong Cuban espresso.

"How did you two meet?" Linc asked, looking at Marisol and Clay.

"Somebody has been anonymously stalking Marisol. I've been acting as her bodyguard and detective."

"How horrible!" Isabel exclaimed, looking from Marisol to Clay in alarm. "Don't you know who it is?"

"It could be Marisol's ex-boyfriend. I won't know until tomorrow when I check the prints. He's in custody right now at the police station."

"You already arrested him?" Linc asked.

Clay nodded. "He tried to kidnap Marisol on a boat last night from the restaurant where we dined when I was on an outdoor phone. When I arrested him, he had the gall to make light of it, insisting it was just a prank."

"Sounds like a nutcase to me." Linc turned to Isabel, who looked panic-stricken. "Don't worry, honey. Marisol will be fine if Clay's protecting her. He's the best detective I ever worked with."

"Thanks," Clay grunted, acknowledging the compliment. "If Gustavo isn't the stalker, then things are going to be a lot more complicated. The AFIS is working on checking his fingerprints nationwide. I'll compare the latent prints I lifted when the AFIS report comes in tomorrow."

"What's the AFIS?" Marisol asked. "That's the first time I've heard you mention it."

"The Automated Fingerprint Identification System," Clay answered.

"If I can help you in any way, let me know," Linc offered. "I know what a heavy load you're carrying."

"OK, but I think I have this under control," Clay said.

"So now you're dating?" Isabel concluded.

"No, we're married," Marisol interjected impulsively. She looked away from Clay, ignoring his pained expression.

Nine

"Married? Congratulations!" Isabel cried, rushing to embrace Clay, then Marisol.

"Wait a minute, Isabel. Marisol hasn't told you the whole story," Clay protested. "We're only married temporarily until I can be sure I've arrested the person who has been stalking her. This guy is so obsessed with marrying her that I felt it would discourage any further threats until I arrest him."

Linc laughed heartily, exchanging amused looks with Isabel. "That's right, Clay, you just keep telling yourself that."

Marisol smiled at Linc, but Clay's tense face warned her that he was unhappy she had mentioned their temporary marriage.

Clay suddenly glanced at his watch and stood up. "It's getting late. Marisol and I have an early morning tomorrow."

"Thank you for a wonderful evening. Everything was delicious," Marisol said, rising beside him. She and Isabel exchanged telephone numbers and said good-bye after Clay promised Linc to keep him abreast of Marisol's case.

On the drive home, Marisol leaned her head

drowsily against Clay's shoulder. "I'm sorry I blurted out that we were married. Are you mad at me?"

"No, I've grown accustomed to expecting the unexpected from you."

Marisol smiled at his gruff admission. "I'm glad you brought me along tonight. Isabel and Linc are so warm and friendly. You really like them, don't you?"

"They're good friends."

They drove the remainder of the distance home in silence, save for the light patter of rainfall. Too emotionally drained to talk anymore, Marisol was content to remain quiet. Witnessing Linc's devotion to his wife and children had triggered a longing for the same from Clay, yet his matter-of-fact explanation for marrying her had dashed her hopes.

When they arrived home, Marisol rushed into the bathroom to wash her face and brush her teeth before changing into an oversized T-shirt. She remembered how much she had ached for Clay's lovemaking before they had left the apartment. But now the last thing she wanted was for Clay to make love to her without telling her the words she wanted to hear. She knew it wouldn't be tonight, but she hoped it would be soon, because she couldn't bear to be intimate with him without a profession of love.

Marisol walked out of the bathroom and stood in the doorway leading from the bedroom to the living room. "Good night, Clay."

"Why are you going to bed so early? Let's watch the news."

"No. I'm too sleepy," she said, pretending to yawn.

"How about a good-night kiss? Come here," he coaxed, patting his lap.

"Not tonight. I'm turning in," she said quietly. "Good night."

For several moments, he studied her beneath hooded eyes. "Good night, *Nena*."

Marisol shivered involuntarily. She wouldn't have liked being called baby by anyone but Clay. Coming from him, it was sweet and incredibly sexy.

Filled with regret, Marisol lay in bed and prayed for sleep to come. She was getting too absorbed in Clay. She needed to go back to work tomorrow and devote her energy to her salon. Her business was booming and she was thankful for that. She had hired top hair stylists and designed a state-of-the-art beauty salon. Many of the area salons were already competing with her success by trying to copy her marketing ideas.

Punching her pillow, she told herself that worrying about Clay wouldn't change a thing until he learned to trust her.

Clay stayed awake long enough to watch the evening news. When it was over, he stripped, then lay down beside Marisol who had fallen asleep with the light on. Lying on her side facing him, she was sleeping deeply, as usual. Clay stroked her cheek, enchanted by the way her eyelashes curled against her cheekbones and her small nose tilted upward against the pillow. Planting a kiss on her soft cheek, he turned off the light.

He had noticed her yearning expression when Linc and Isabel had kissed their children good night. Marisol probably longed for a family life like theirs. As much as it pained Clay to admit, she would have to settle for not having a baby if she stayed with him. Her pledge of fidelity had deeply moved him. In essence, Marisol had said she would love him unconditionally. No woman, especially not Jillian, had ever uttered those words to him.

Yet Clay still had problems with trust in marriage. Even to someone as desirable and sweet as Marisol. His years alone had made him relish the solitude, but he could already feel her presence chipping away at his resolve. From the first moment he had made love to her, he had felt fiercely possessive. Clay gazed at Marisol's sleeping face with a heavy burden of regret in his heart.

Her kind words earlier that day floated into his mind. *"If I had been Jillian, I would have been delighted to have your baby. I have enough love in my heart for all types of children."* God, how he wanted to believe her, to trust that she was different from any other woman in his life, but he knew better. He would never blindly trust a woman again.

Marisol awoke Monday morning determined to face the day with a positive attitude. She regretted her gloomy mood at the end of the wonderful Sunday she and Clay had spent together. Every time she thought about Linc and Isabel's family life, she pined for a close relationship with Clay, like theirs. How would she ever be able to convince Clay that he could trust in her love; that she would happily have children with him without worrying about handicaps?

Just yesterday she'd impulsively promised him that she would remain at his side as long as he wanted her.

But that was before she'd met Linc and Isabel, before witnessing their unconditional love. Marisol knew she needed more from Clay. There was no problem with their physical bond; what was flawed was his emotional involvement.

Once again, she told herself to be patient. Somehow she'd have to convince him that he could trust her, especially after Jillian's betrayal. Marisol pulled herself upright and squared her shoulders as she made a crucial decision. She was tired of moping about Clay's attitude toward marriage and babies. She would find a way to teach him to love wholeheartedly again. Cheered by her new determination to woo and conquer Clay's reticence, Marisol joined him in the kitchen for breakfast.

"I think I'll skip my workout today," she said. "I want to open the salon early."

Clay glanced at her with an odd expression. "I'm surprised you're up already."

"I had a restless night."

"So did I. Probably for different reasons." He seemed on edge as his dark, unswerving gaze penetrated hers from across the table.

She stood up. "I have to get ready."

"I'll read the paper while you shower."

Marisol hurried through her shower and styled her mousse-dampened hair with her fingertips as she blew it dry. She wanted to get to the salon as soon as possible. That way she would have time alone to sort out her thoughts.

When they were dressed and ready to leave, Clay followed Marisol's car to the salon. "I'll be back at seven to escort you home," he said, just before driving off.

"I don't think that's necessary now that you've arrested Gustavo."

"Wait for me at seven," he said, undeterred.

Marisol gave in only because she was anxious to leave. "All right. Go to work and stop telling me what to do."

"Be careful. Call me if anything comes up," he said before driving away.

Marisol entered her beauty salon and scanned it with a surge of satisfaction. The pink-and-black-neo art-deco look had paid off; her clients often commented about the beautiful surroundings. In the center of the main room was an island counter with a large mirror surrounded by flattering studio lights where Jessie, the makeup artist, did make-overs. Marisol had a special room set aside for waxing and facials to the right of the main salon. At the back, next to the supply room, was a small kitchen where the capuccino and espresso machines seemed to be in constant use. She strongly believed in pampering her clients so they'd keep coming back.

Feeling especially energetic, Marisol worked tirelessly all morning. Her schedule was relatively light in the morning, but booked solid in the afternoon. She made good use of the time before her first appointment to check the cleanliness of the kitchen, the changing booths and the bathroom. She reminded the shampoo girls to make sure there were plenty of clean towels and to restock shampoo and conditioner supplies every morning before the first customers arrived.

But when Marisol checked the cash register, she was shocked to find no money. She scanned the drawer beneath the register where they kept small change and found that it too was empty. Even when she made bank deposits, Marisol always made sure there was enough change in the cash register for her morning clients. Puzzled, she remembered she had shut off the burglar alarm that morning when she'd entered, and there had been no sign of forced entry. She briefly wondered if she'd been robbed. A chill passed through Marisol as she dialed Trini's apartment. She was surprised to hear a man answer and say that Trini had just left.

Marisol postponed her next appointment and dashed to the bank next door. She withdrew one hundred dollars to supply change for her patrons and returned to the salon to cut and style her first client's hair. She decided to question Trini before calling the police to report the theft. Moments later, Trini finally walked in, sporting a black eye.

Marisol instantly suspected it might have been Ray who answered the telephone when she'd called Trini that morning. A few months back, he'd introduced himself as the owner of a competing salon in the same area and had made a move on some of the hair stylists. Marisol couldn't see what attraction Ray held for Trini, who had started a relationship with him right away. Ray, a short, muscular man, might have been considered passable if it hadn't been for his abrasive personality and bulldog appearance. Marisol had been turned off at the outset by his sexual innuendos and sexist remarks.

Trini had eventually moved in with Ray, hoping he would marry her. She'd once confided in Marisol that he only beat her when he drank too much. Shortly afterward, he battered Trini so viciously that she'd landed in the hospital emergency room. Marisol hadn't been able to convince Trini to press charges against Ray, but she succeeded in getting her to leave him and temporarily move in with her.

"We need to talk," Marisol said. "Let's go to the supply room."

"What's wrong?" Trini asked.

When they reached the supply room, out of her clients' hearing distance, Marisol asked, "First of all, what happened to your eye?"

"I tripped in the dark last night and bumped my face against the dresser."

Yeah, right, Marisol thought to herself. "The last time you had a black eye was when Ray beat you up. It sounded like Ray when I called you. Are you seeing him again?"

Trini shuddered. "No way. I have a new boyfriend."

"I hope you're telling me the truth about Ray. Especially after that last beating!" Marisol took a deep breath before exhaling it. "Now, where's the cash that's missing from the register? It was empty when I came in this morning. Did you take the cash home with you on Saturday to make a deposit?"

"Yes. But I only deposited the checks at the bank this morning before coming in." Trini looked down sheepishly. "I'm sorry, Marisol. I had to borrow some money because I needed groceries. You can take the hundred dollars out of my next paycheck."

"Trini, if you don't get your act together there won't be another paycheck. I can't believe you'd do something like that. How am I going to trust you now?"

"Give me another chance," Trini pleaded. "I promise it won't happen again."

"See that it doesn't or I will have to let you go." Trini walked to the door. "Wait, don't leave yet," Marisol said. "Why did you tell Gustavo I'd be at Scotty's Saturday night? Especially when I obviously didn't want to see him?"

Trini's face flushed with embarrassment. "It just slipped out."

"I hope I can count on you to think before you speak, especially in light of the stalker."

"Clay will watch over you now that you're married." Trini looked truly contrite when she asked, "Are you still mad enough to fire me?"

Marisol would have to be heartless to fire Trini, looking the way she did with her puffy eye. "No, I'm not going to fire you, but I will if something like this ever happens again. Now go and do Anne's manicure. She wants a full set of tips. That should bring in at least sixty dollars. I'll start deducting what you owe me from that."

"Thanks, Marisol." Trini put on her sunglasses and sat down at her station.

The only highlight of the afternoon was the return of Marisol's closest friend and star hair stylist, Nuri Ramos, from her honeymoon.

"Nuri, you look great!" Marisol exclaimed. "You're tanned and positively glowing."

"You're looking pretty good yourself. What have you been up to?"

"Lots of things. But first tell me about yourself. How was Aruba?"

"Awesome." Nuri flashed a naughty grin. "So was Omar."

Marisol chuckled. "I'm glad you're back. I missed you. But why did you come in a day earlier than expected?"

"Because of you. While I was flying back, I got a weird feeling and started to panic thinking about the guy who's been bothering you. Then I tried calling you several times at night and only got your recording. I drove to your apartment, but you weren't there, so I decided to come in early and check on you here."

"I'm sorry I worried you. You're a good friend." She moved a little closer to Nuri and whispered, "I think Gustavo might be the stalker."

"Gustavo?" Nuri repeated. "I've suspected him all along."

"Marisol, there's a phone call for you," Luz shouted. "It's Mr. Guitierrez."

Marisol ran to the telephone. She spoke to him briefly and returned to Nuri's side with a satisfied smile.

"What did he want?" Nuri asked.

"This is amazing. He said I could renew the lease and that he wasn't going to raise my rent as high as he had threatened last week."

"You can thank me for that," Trini chimed in.

Marisol turned to stare at Trini. "Why? What did you do?"

"I told him that you had hired a lawyer and were contemplating suing him," Trini said smugly.

"You shouldn't have done that, Trini!" Marisol exclaimed, exasperated. "I was going to get Clay to use his legal knowledge to help me deal with him."

"So I beat you to it. It worked, didn't it? Maybe now you won't be mad at me anymore."

"Would you believe I never got around to discussing the lease with Clay even though we're married?" She turned to Nuri in a low voice. "Let me get back to Gustavo . . .", she began.

"Stop," Nuri interrupted, throwing up her hands. "Do you think you can casually mention getting married and then change the subject? You'd better fill me in on this marriage. Just who is Clay?"

"It's a long story. I'll tell you about Clay later," Marisol whispered. "Now, about Gustavo . . ."

"Forget it, *chica*," Nuri interjected. "Tell me about Clay. When did you meet him?"

Marisol glanced around her and noticed every ear in the room was cocked eagerly for the latest juicy morsel of gossip. "I can't talk about it now. I'll call you tonight and fill you in on everything," she said, ignoring the collective groan of disappointment.

"I'll hold you to it. Now, put me to work," Nuri said.

"You mean you're staying?" Marisol asked hopefully.

"I've been lying on this round behind all week at the beach. It'll do me good to stand and style some hair. My hands are just itching for scissors."

"Great. I could use a break this afternoon to run some errands. I'll call my customers and tell them you're back from your honeymoon. I'm sure they won't mind switching their appointments to you."

"Call them now," Nuri urged. "If you want to take the rest of the day off, I'll close shop for you and make the deposit."

"Thanks, you're a lifesaver." Before leaving, she briefly filled Nuri in on her problems with Trini and warned her to keep at an eye on her. After calling Clay to inform him that she'd meet him at home, Marisol left, feeling like a load had been taken off her shoulders. When Nuri was left in charge, the salon always ran smoothly. She was honest and liked by the other stylists as well as the clients.

With mounting frustration, Clay drove home from work. His jaw clenched in disgust as he remembered Gustavo's attitude when Clay had released him that afternoon due to insufficient evidence. None of the latent fingerprints Clay had lifted from Marisol's apartment had matched Gustavo's. The AFIS report hadn't confirmed anything either. Gustavo had no previous record of arrests, and his statement that he'd arrived in Miami the previous week was corroborated by Mexicana Airlines.

The only conclusive information that had come in today was that the red satin handcuffs and the Barbie dress had been sewn on the same sewing machine with an identical stitch. The analysis on the handcuffs had shown that they were custom-made by an expert tailor.

Clay clutched the steering wheel and relived his last conversation with Gustavo when he'd warned him not to go near Marisol again. He'd had to physically restrain himself from hitting Gustavo when he'd replied that Marisol wasn't worth the effort.

Clay's compulsion to stop the stalker went far beyond his loyalty to Marcos. In his mind's eye, he kept seeing Marisol's bleak expression when she'd stood in the bedroom doorway last night. Guilt that he couldn't share her dreams of having a family gnawed at him, but he wouldn't give her false hopes.

Even though Marisol had said she'd never worry

about having a mentally handicapped child, Clay knew that it was human nature to worry about such things and that she might change her mind if she became pregnant. He would never be able to bear being the source of her apprehension, to see the worry in her eyes and know that she would want to shield him from it.

Ten

When he arrived at the condo, Clay unlocked the door and flung it open. "Thank God you're still here." He pulled Marisol into his arms, holding her against his chest as he smoothed her hair away from her forehead and kissed the top of her head.

She stepped back from his tight embrace. "Where else would I be? Has something happened that I don't know about?"

Clay shook his head. "Ever since you went on that little excursion to the beach, I've worried about leaving you alone, even for a short while."

Marisol sank down on the sofa. "Gee, it's nice to see how much you trust me. I told you I was sorry about that."

"OK, I'll try not to bring it up again," Clay said, the corners of his mouth quirking upward. "How was your day?"

Marisol shrugged. "Good and bad. The good part is that Nuri returned from her honeymoon."

Clay joined her on the sofa. "Who's Nuri?"

"My closest friend. She came in a day earlier because she couldn't reach me and was worried that something had happened."

"Sounds like a good friend."

"She's the best. I left Nuri in charge of the salon and came home early today. When she's there I know everything will run smoothly. Unfortunately, I can't say the same about Trini."

"Why not?"

"Trini did the dumbest thing over the weekend while I was away. She borrowed all the money from the cash register without asking my permission."

Clay's brows drew together, forming a stern line. "Borrowed is a pretty mild word for stealing," he observed caustically.

"I don't think she was stealing. Sometimes Trini doesn't use common sense."

"Then why is she still working for you?"

"She's the best nail technician I've hired. Plus she's beautiful and exotic-looking. But despite all that, she has low self-esteem. And her personal finances are a mess."

Clay's jaw jutted forward. "She doesn't sound like an ideal employee to me."

"Trini has other qualities that make her ideal. She's a perfectionist at her manicures and she puts in long hours at work."

Clay's disgruntled expression showed he wasn't convinced.

"The beauty business is very different from the law-enforcement profession, Blackthorne. I look for different qualities when I hire people. I think anyone who has the right look and attitude, along with the job expertise, deserves a chance to prove herself—especially if she's a hard worker."

"That's very democratic of you, but not very practical. I'm going to conduct a background check on your employees. I'll need their names and social security numbers."

"Is that necessary? They're not only my employees, they're my friends, too. What Trini did was foolish, but I don't think that warrants an investigation."

"I know what I'm doing."

"Then I'd better tell you that Trini has a previous record for shoplifting."

Clay's brows shot up. "You hired Trini knowing that she's dishonest?"

"She's not dishonest, she's just had a rough life. Her mother was a single parent who waitressed and danced in a seedy bar. Trini was sixteen when she was caught shoplifting. She told me she had only done it to get a decent outfit so she could apply for a job after school. She also said that she has never done anything illegal since then. And I believe her."

Clay crossed his arms and stared at her in disbelief.

"Don't look at me that way. I told you, I believe in giving people a second chance. Trini was honest enough to tell me about her past shortly after I hired her. If she hadn't, I probably would have never found out."

"That doesn't change the fact that she stole from you."

"Haven't you been listening to me? She borrowed it to buy groceries. I've already deducted the amount from her paycheck." Marisol sighed. "I think she's gotten back together with her old boyfriend, Ray. He's such a louse."

"Why?"

"Ray is rough with her, emotionally and physically. He once beat Trini so badly that she had to be hospitalized. She moved in with me temporarily so she could hide from him while she healed. Before she moved out, I got Trini to threaten Ray with a restraining order if he didn't leave her alone."

"Did he back off?"

"Yes. He had just moved to Miami and I'm sure he wanted to avoid problems with the police," she said.

Clay grimaced. "Only cowards beat up on women. I've seen a good share of them. What does Ray do for a living?"

"He owns a beauty salon near mine. When he first came in to the salon, I thought he might be checking out the competition."

"Add his full name to the list of your employees so I can check him out too."

"You'll have to wait until tomorrow. That information is at the salon."

"Don't forget, or we'll have to go back for it tomorrow."

Marisol looked heavenward and sighed out loud. "You're a real slave driver, Blackthorne."

The following day, Marisol couldn't shake the feeling that she was being watched. From the moment she arrived at work, she felt like she needed to be constantly looking over her shoulder. She hadn't realized just how much Luz's brush with death had affected her until she returned to work, away from Clay's constant presence.

At lunchtime, Marisol decided to drive to a nearby deli for lunch. As she approached her car she noticed that the tire on the driver's side was slashed and the window on the same side was shattered. She looked inside her car. A large white rock with the word "WHORE" spray painted in red letters sat on the tiny fragments of glass covering the driver's seat. Filled with helpless rage, she glanced around her to see if anyone had witnessed the vandalism.

A hefty woman approached Marisol, a horrified expression on her florid face. "Is that what the crashing noise was? Who did this?"

"I don't know."

"I have a cellular phone if you want to call the police."

"No, thanks. I'll call from the Villabella Beauty Salon."

When the woman left, Marisol slumped against the side of her car. Tremors shook her shoulders and before long, she was sobbing uncontrollably. She wasn't aware of how long she stood there crying before she felt strong arms surround her. Clay's masculine scent enveloped her.

"*Nena,* are you hurt?" Clay asked, his deep voice anxious.

Marisol fought to regain her composure. "Clay!" Bewildered, she stepped back to peer at him through misty eyes. "How did you know I was in trouble?"

"I stopped by to have lunch with you. When I pulled into the parking lot, I saw you leaning against the car with your face buried in your hands. You almost took twenty years off my life."

"Look at what he did to my car!" she said, gesturing wildly.

"When did this happen?"

"I don't know. I hate falling apart like this, but today I'm really spooked."

"You're only human, Marisol." Clay kissed her damp face, then pulled a clean handkerchief from his back pocket. "Here. Blow your nose."

After she blew her nose, Marisol peered inside her

car again. "I have to call a mechanic. There's no way I'll be able to get all this glass out!"

"I'll take care of it. Go inside the salon and I'll meet you there with lunch once I've questioned a few people and filled out a report."

Clay returned an hour later and joined Marisol in the kitchen, where she sat talking with Nuri.

"Nuri, this is my husband, Clay."

Clay nodded and shook Nuri's proffered hand. "Nice meeting you, Nuri. I hope you don't mind that I need to speak privately with Marisol."

"No problem," Nuri said. "I'll catch you later, Marisol."

Clay settled into a chair beside her. "You still look shaky."

"I've had a weird feeling since this morning. Like I'm being followed. I can't shake this premonition that something terrible is about to happen."

"You need twenty-four hour protection and I can't provide that if I want to keep my job. I have other cases I'm working on. I'll look into assigning an additional bodyguard for the times when I can't watch over you."

"I can't work with someone hovering over me."

Even though Clay remained silent, Marisol knew he disagreed and would probably assign someone to tail her anyway.

The next morning, Clay and Marisol left for work early. He had a backlog of information to review and she had morning appointments to take care of. Everything at the salon started out fine until Nuri came to her with a worried expression.

"Can we talk privately in the supply room?" Nuri asked.

"Of course. What's wrong?" Marisol asked when they entered the room.

"Look." Nuri pointed to an empty shelf. "I think Trini has been stealing more things," Nuri said, her worried eyes scanning the shelves. "Two curling irons, five styling brushes, and at least three perm kits are missing."

"When did you notice they were gone?"

"Just now, when I came to get a perm kit. I started checking the supplies and I noticed the other missing items. Trini came to work yesterday carrying a small black suitcase. When we asked her about it, she said it contained a change of clothes for a date," Nuri said. "But she never changed her clothes before she left last night."

"Surely Trini must have known she'd be suspected and caught," Marisol said.

"What are you two talking about?"

Marisol and Nuri whirled around as Trini entered the room.

"Marisol will tell you," Nuri said, exiting quickly.

"Some supplies are missing from this shelf since last night, Trini." Marisol leveled a sharp look at her. "Did you take them?"

"Why do you always suspect *me?* Are you planning to tell your detective husband?" she asked, her brow furrowed with fear.

"I don't remember telling you that Clay is a detective."

Trini shrugged. "Gustavo mentioned it."

"Are you seeing Gustavo?" Marisol asked.

"Why do you care? You're married now."

"That's right. I'm also trying to run a successful business. I've given you enough chances, Trini."

Trini's eyes filled with tears. "It's not my fault."

"Of course it is. Why did you do it?"

"I needed some things."

"That's a poor excuse and you know it. It's almost as if you wanted to get caught, Trini. You've become so self-destructive! You know I won't be able to give you a good reference for your next job. It's not the missing supplies I'm upset about; it's your lies. They've destroyed my trust in you."

"I'll replace what I took. Please don't call the police!"

Marisol sighed. "The only way I'll consider that is if you promise me you'll go for counseling immediately."

"I promise."

"I'll want proof from you," Marisol warned.

Trini nodded. "So you won't call the police?"

"Not if you can prove you're getting help."

Trini let out a breath of relief. "Thanks, Marisol. You're a good person."

Marisol refused to soften, despite Trini's forlorn expression. "You can't continue working here. Please clean out your position and give me back the salon keys. I want you to leave immediately."

With slumped shoulders, Trini walked out of the room and dismantled her private belongings from her position. After tearfully returning the keys, she walked out of the salon, leaving the other employees stunned at her dishonesty.

Marisol had planned on a free afternoon, but now she'd have to fill in for Trini, in order not to have to cancel her bookings and deal with irate customers. She felt betrayed by Trini's treachery. Not only had

Marisol trusted her, but she'd given her a second chance after she'd stolen the cash from the register.

Marisol had noticed an ill-concealed dark bruise on Trini's wrist when she'd reached up to wipe her eyes. She was sure now more than ever that Trini was back together with Ray. Reflecting on it, Marisol realized that Trini had been acting irrationally since the day she'd walked in with a black eye.

The stalker remained silent and inactive for the rest of the weekend, further distressing Marisol. The more he stayed hidden, the harder it would be to catch him. Clay had told Marisol that when he conducted a background check on her employees and Ray Campbell, everyone had checked out clean. She could tell Clay was making a special effort not to mention the stalker even though his eyes showed a wariness that boded danger.

By Monday morning, Marisol felt desperate for a change. During her lunch break, she sat beside Nuri in the kitchen. "I'm going nuts worrying about the stalker and waiting to see what happens next. I need to do something active. I've been toying with the idea of expanding this salon into a day spa."

Nuri's eyes widened. "Really? Where did that come from?"

"I've been accumulating some information on beauty spa management and it sounds like a fun way to increase our profits. When I turn thirty this December, I'll receive the rest of the inheritance *mi abuelito* left me. Then I'll be able to find a new location instead of renewing my lease here."

"With all the money here in SoBe, your spa should be a hit. How can I help?"

"Would you like to manage it?"

Nuri hugged Marisol. "I'd love to!"

"You're the best person for the job. I hadn't signed up for a seminar because I didn't think the timing was right before. But now I need to shift gears and start something new."

"How does Clay feel about your sudden decision?"

"I haven't told him, since he's so focused on protecting me from the stalker. As soon as I call Blanca about replacing Trini, I'm going home to catch up with some personal things."

"Blanca? Have I met her?"

"She's a Nicaraguan woman who inquired about a job here a couple of months ago. She's a meticulous nail technician and she's bilingual, too."

Before leaving the apartment that morning, Marisol told Clay that she'd be working late because she had to cover Trini's appointments until she hired someone. But when Blanca agreed to start working immediately, Marisol left Nuri in charge and departed soon afterward. She stopped her car beside a street vendor and purchased a bunch of daisies, then hurried home.

Pulling into the parking lot, Marisol looked into her rearview mirror before exiting the car. Relieved that she was alone, she got out with her stun gun in hand. She greeted Alan, the security guard, on her way inside.

Back at Clay's apartment, Marisol placed the fresh daisies in a vase. She craved a nice, warm bath to soothe her tired feet. After her bath, she slathered scented body cream on her skin. She wanted to be soft and fragrant for Clay's arrival.

Tonight would be special. After his weary day, she would give him a massage, returning the wonderful full body massage he'd given her last week. She would lovingly encourage Clay to show her the scar she was sure he was hiding. Only then would he be freed of that hang-up. Tonight it would be her turn to pamper him.

Relishing the thought, she slipped into her bathrobe and padded barefoot into the bedroom. Folding down the comforter, she settled into bed for a brief nap.

When Clay arrived at his apartment building that afternoon, he intercepted Marcos at the front door. "Hi, what are you doing here?" Clay asked, surprised.

"Che," Marcos greeted him, heartily clapping him on the back. "I called you at the precinct, but Jenny told me you left for home early." He walked into the elevator beside Clay. "How's Marisol?"

"She's OK. She's still at work."

"Good. What's the update on the stalker?"

"I assigned an undercover officer to watch over Marisol when I can't be with her, while I work on following some leads."

"Has she received more threats?"

"She did for a while, but the stalker is laying low now."

"Do you have any leads on who it is yet?" Marcos asked as they exited the elevator on Clay's floor.

Clay led the way to the apartment. "I've ruled out Gustavo. Even though I arrested him last Saturday night when he kidnapped Marisol on a speedboat, I don't think he's the stalker anymore."

"What! Did he harm her?" Marcos thundered.

"No, I caught up with them just in time. Gustavo was unarmed, but God only knows what he might have tried."

Clay opened the door and invited Marcos inside.

Hands braced behind his back, Marcos paced the living room floor. "Tell me about the kidnapping."

"Sure. Sit down."

When they were sprawled on the leather couches in the living room, Clay said, "Gustavo told Marisol that he pulled the prank because he was afraid she wouldn't agree to meet with him otherwise. He still loves her and hopes to get back together."

"That's ridiculous. *Ese imbécil* better stay away from her," Marcos muttered, his square jaw clenching with menace.

"Gustavo was scared spitless in jail, enough not to bother her again."

"How can you be sure he's not the stalker?"

"None of the evidence I've gathered supports it. Gustavo doesn't fit the pattern of a typical stalker either. It has to be someone else. But that wasn't the only event of the week. Marisol's receptionist, Luz, was the victim of a hit-and-run accident. Afterward, Marisol received a message threatening that she'd be the next victim. That's when she finally agreed to marry me for appearances' sake." He paused. "And later this week her car window was smashed by a rock with the word "whore" painted on it."

Marcos shouted an expletive. "Why didn't you tell me what's been happening?"

"There was no need to alarm you. Marisol's under my protection now," Clay reminded him. He narrowly missed saying "Marisol's mine now" instead.

Marcos's gaze was penetrating as he looked at Clay with new eyes. "Are you two involved?" he asked bluntly.

"It's impossible not to get involved with Marisol. She's so full of life. I have to admit she's gotten under my skin," Clay replied, feeling that rush of warmth she brought into his life.

Marcos thought about it a few seconds. "I'm glad. It couldn't have happened to a better man," Marcos said, grinning.

"Yeah, well, she really needs a keeper. You know how friendly she is. She trusts everybody and wants to believe the best about them."

"What do you mean?"

"She had to fire Trini over the weekend for stealing," Clay said. "Your sister actually gave Trini a second chance after she admitted to stealing a hundred dollars from the cash register. Then Trini blew it by stealing supplies over the weekend."

Marcos didn't seem surprised. "I met Trini shortly after Marisol hired her and she didn't impress me. I hope that's the last of her." His eyes crinkled briefly, reminding Clay of Marisol's hazel eyes. Only hers were lighter, with green specks in the irises. "Tell me how it went when Marisol gave you the haircut. Did she torment you very much?"

"Please don't remind me," Clay retorted, grimacing.

Marcos chuckled as Clay retold Marisol's antics with the mashed avocado. By the time Clay finished relating his first experience with Marisol, including the stungun incident, he and Marcos were laughing out loud.

Marisol groggily turned on her side. She opened her eyes and wondered if she was dreaming. She was sure she heard Clay's deep rumbling laughter and someone else's.

Marcos!

She sat up, wide awake now, and concentrated on

the voices coming from the living room. As she tip-toed to the door, she went numb with shock when she overheard Marcos and Clay. They were laughing at her expense!

"Does she know who you are yet, Che?" Marcos asked.

"No, and it hasn't been easy lying to her or hiding this tattoo," Clay admitted, thumping his chest.

Marisol burst into the room with the strength of a rampaging tornado. She ripped Clay's shirt open, sending buttons scattering on the tile floor.

"You're *el Che!*" she yelled, staring at the serpent tattoo etched on Clay's smooth, brown chest.

Clay stepped back from her. "Hey! You just ruined a perfectly good shirt!"

"Too bad! All this time I felt compassion for you because I thought you were hiding a scar." She pointed to the front door. "Get out, both of you!"

Marcos reached out to ruffle Marisol's hair. *"Vale, mocosa,* settle down. It was my idea. I can explain everything."

Marisol darted out of his reach. "You have a lot to account for Marcos, but right now I don't even want to hear your voice."

"Marisol, *por favor!"* Marcos protested.

"How dare you both sit there so smugly, laughing at me behind my back!" she raged.

"Sunshine, calm down and listen to me," Clay inter-vened.

"Sunshine?" Marcos asked in a slightly amused tone.

Marisol ignored Marcos. "Why should I listen to you, *Che?* You've done nothing but lie to me from the beginning." She stormed into the bedroom closet, slamming the door behind her.

She heard Clay and Marcos's footsteps as they approached.

"Don't open this door!" Marisol yelled. There was no time to get dressed. After searching frantically in the closet, she remembered she had left her purse on the kitchen counter. She ran past Clay and Marcos, who waited by the closet door with flabbergasted expressions on their faces.

Grabbing her purse, she yanked the bouquet of daisies out of the vase and returned to the living room. Clay and Marcos stood blocking her exit through the front door.

"Let me by!" she demanded.

"Not until you listen to me," Clay said calmly.

Marisol jabbed Clay's solid midsection with the dripping daisies. "You can talk to these." She glared at the towering men in front of her. "Move aside or I'll hate you forever."

"Let her go. I'll follow her to her apartment," Clay said.

"Don't bother! I'll call the security guard," she said.

Clay put his hands on her shoulders. "Stop it, Marisol. You're hysterical."

"Tough!" she retorted, pushing his hands from her shoulders. She yanked open the door and bolted out of Clay's apartment barefooted. Marisol ran down the hall and stepped into the open elevator, managing to close the elevator doors before Clay could reach them.

At her apartment, Marisol opened the new locks on her door and darted inside, carefully relocking the door. She turned on the C.D. player and pumped up

the volume full blast to drown out the protests screaming from her wounded heart.

Clay had deceived her! So had Marcos. But she
wasn't nearly as angry with Marcos as she was furious
with Clay. She was used to Marcos getting involved in
her life uninvited. But Clay? How could he have betrayed her trust like that? She had repeatedly told him
how she felt about being treated like a baby by Marcos's constant smothering.

Realization dawned painfully. Clay had never really
loved her. He had only protected her as a favor to
Marcos. How could she have been so blind? The clues
had all been lined up for her to analyze. From the beginning, Clay had been reluctant to disclose that he
was a detective. And most telling of all, he had never
appeared bare chested in front of her, despite their intimate lovemaking.

All that effort to hide his tattoo! How much
longer had he expected to carry on the farce? To
think she had sympathized that he was shy about a
horrible scar on his body, when in reality he had
been shielding her from noticing he had the identical tattoo she'd seen on Marcos's chest on many occasions.

Her heart clenched painfully as she recalled the
sound of Clay's and Marcos's laughter that afternoon.
Nobody would make a fool out of her again, she
vowed, sick at heart. First Gustavo, then Trini, and
now Clay. Wasn't there anyone left whom she cared
about who hadn't lied to her?

Marisol pressed her hands against her temples and
squeezed her eyes shut in an attempt to negate the
many endearments she had lavished on Clay. What a
stupid fool she had been to hope that he loved her

when he'd only been doing his duty! Clay must have felt so indebted to Marcos, that he had been willing to sacrifice his independence to marry his naive little sister, just to watch over her.

And what about his tender lovemaking? Had that too been part of his gratitude? She suddenly hated Clay and his lies. How could he have made love to her without realizing she had given him her whole heart and soul? Her feelings of violation by the stalker's threats paled next to her feelings of betrayal at Clay's deception.

He was no longer her hero.

He was a deceitful liar.

Clay rang the doorbell to Marisol's apartment. After waiting a minute for her to answer, he knocked on the door. He could hear loud music blaring in her apartment. When several moments passed with no response, Clay banged on the door with his fist. "Marisol, open up!"

"Go away!" she shouted back. "I'm sick of your lies!"

"Give me a chance to explain."

She yanked open the door. "How could you think you could get away with such a brazen lie? I don't want to see you ever again. Now leave." She tried to close the door in Clay's face but his hand shot out to stop her, infuriating her even more.

Hands braced on his hips, Clay leaned forward to glare at Marisol, eye to eye. His black eyes blazed a scalding path to her equally sparking eyes. "The hell I will! I'm not going anywhere until we've resolved this."

"There's nothing to resolve," she said, and forced herself to regain her composure. She had already lost it in Clay's apartment and she had no intention of letting him see her frazzled again. "You are officially off this case."

"Not until I arrest the stalker."

"I'll hire somebody else. I'm sure Linc can recommend an *honest* detective."

"Linc wouldn't do anything I disagree with." He crossed his arms over his chest and leaned against the door frame.

"Then I'll hire a private investigator. Either way, I want you out of my life. I've had enough lies for one lifetime." Marisol walked away from him and headed to the bedroom. Clay closed the door behind him and followed her inside. She gathered her purse and keys, ignoring Clay as he shadowed her every move.

Clay gently turned Marisol to face him. *"Nena,* the only reason I didn't admit to knowing Marcos is because he warned me you'd refuse my help. He told me how you felt about his interfering in your life. I never meant to hurt your feelings."

"Hurt my feelings? Is that what you think you've done?" she whispered brokenly. "No, Clay, you haven't just hurt my feelings, you've broken my heart!"

Clay flinched and dropped his hands from her stiff shoulders. "Marisol, it started out as a favor to Marcos, but I have grown to care for you."

Marisol's heart contracted painfully. He hadn't said he had grown to love her—just that he'd grown to care for her. Heck, she cared for her friends, but she loved Clay. When he had made love to her after Gustavo's kidnapping he'd said, *"You're mine Marisol. I'm pos-*

sessive. Even after I arrest the stalker. You're mine."
Had those been lies, too?

Facing Clay squarely, Marisol tried to keep the sharp disillusionment from her voice. "I told you once that I would stay by you as long as you wanted me there. I'm sorry, but I no longer feel that way. I know now I can never be happy in your kind of relationship. I want to marry someone who loves me and wants a real marriage. Just one child would make me happy." She took off his mother's ring and handed it to Clay. "Here, I won't be needing this anymore."

Clay grabbed her hand and replaced the ring on her finger. "We still have to look like we're married while I'm on the case."

"I can't even bear to look at you, Clay. There's no way I'd be able to live in your apartment any longer. Especially after knowing you protected me only because you had promised Marcos."

He ran a ragged hand through his coarse hair. "I already told you it only started out that way. I can't bear the thought of anyone hurting you."

"Why? Because it would disappoint Marcos?"

"Stop it," he bit out. "If you won't believe I care for you and you still insist on a strictly platonic relationship, then so be it. But I'm staying on the case until I arrest the stalker."

"Suit yourself." She turned away with an indifferent shrug. "I intend to move my things out of your apartment by this evening."

Clay ground his teeth. "All right. I'll help you move out. But you'd better get used to the idea that I'm not giving up."

She whirled around to face him. Fury mushroomed

inside of her again at his obstinate words. "You won't like the new me, Clay. I've been a trusting dope all my life, but not anymore. You've destroyed my trust in you. There are too many beautiful things in life to enjoy and wonderful people to share them with." She clutched her keys and stomped to the door. "I want to start bringing my things back now. Has Marcos left already?"

"Yes." He exhaled wearily. "I'll call him tonight."

"Good, because I don't want to talk to him."

Clay waited for Marisol to change out of her bathrobe, then followed her to his apartment.

"I understand how you feel, Marisol, and I'm sorry. I promise I won't keep the truth from you," he said, once they were inside his place.

Clay looked so remorseful that Marisol was tempted to forgive him on the spot, but she didn't. He needed to realize she deserved honesty. "I don't trust your promises."

"I've been patiently trying to explain the reasons why I had to lie to you, but you haven't listened to any of them."

"Yes, I have. I just can't accept them."

Clay sat down on the couch. He braced his elbows on his knees as he clasped his hands and seemed to ponder what to say. "Marisol, your life is still in danger," he said grimly. "I'm the best man for the job. We have to stay married until I catch the stalker. After that I'll give you the divorce you want."

"If I agree to this, you have to follow *my* ground rules."

Clay roughly rubbed the back of his neck. "What are they?"

"First of all, we'll live in my apartment. I can't

bear to live here any longer playing the adoring bride to you." That comment seemed to cut him to the quick.

"Secondly, you don't touch me anymore. Not even in public."

"Is that it?" Tight-lipped, Clay said, "It will be hell living beside you and not being able to touch you. But I'll agree to anything now—just to keep you safe."

"The most important ground rule is that you don't attempt to seduce me."

Clay let out an exasperated groan. "That's understood. How can I seduce you if I can't even touch you?" he groused.

"Your eyes alone can seduce me," she muttered, before realizing it. The last thing she wanted was for Clay to know that she was still vulnerable to him.

"It's a deal." Clay shook her hand briefly. "Sorry, I forgot about promising not to touch you," he said, dimples deepening into a slow grin.

Marisol looked away. One look at Clay's heart-stopping dimples could melt a stone. Even his smile seemed to mock her resolve, but she wouldn't let him back into her heart until he got down on his knees and pledged his love to her. And not a moment before.

Marisol took great pains to avoid Clay at all costs. She made sure not to eat breakfast or dinner with him and worked late hours at the shop, ignoring his car as he protectively followed her to and from work.

Nighttime was the worst. She had conceded that he could sleep next to her, but that was torture. She would lie awake staring at his sleeping face or get up and pace the living room until she could compose herself enough to return and resume her futile attempt at sleep.

Yet every time Marisol remembered Clay's motives for his involvement with her, her resolve strengthened. The arrangement was wearing Clay down, too. He was often irritable and edgy, eating little and sleeping fitfully. They only conversed when necessary now. The blossoming friendship they had enjoyed during their intimacy was now strained as they kept themselves physically and emotionally alienated from each other.

The following week dragged on until Saturday with no further communication from the stalker. Marisol wondered if the stalker had decided to give up on her since he knew she was married and probably knew that Clay was a police detective. Clay no longer attempted small talk with her, withdrawing even more. Yet he stayed by her side relentlessly when he wasn't at work. Even when he studied, she knew that Clay was preoccupied with the stalker and when he might strike again.

Marisol felt anxious to resume her normal lifestyle. It pained her to admit that there was no real future with Clay. As much as she loved him, if they didn't have the same life goals, it would never work.

Every day Marisol was obliged to wear his mother's ring was just one more reminder that it was on loan. The wonderful wedding night they had spent in the hotel had become a bittersweet memory that Marisol didn't allow herself to dwell on anymore. She admitted that Clay was an honorable man. His strong sense of integrity must have compelled him to uphold his promise to Marcos. Clay would have said or done anything to complete his pledge.

Even make beautiful love to her, she thought with a surge of sadness.

Sunday morning, Clay received an urgent phone call from Jimmy. He walked into the bedroom to find Marisol still asleep.

Her complexion glowed a soft peach color and her mouth, relaxed and vulnerable, invited kissing. She lay still, clutching a pillow to her side. Clay envied the pillow its proximity to Marisol's tantalizing, T-shirt-clad body. Her tanned legs beckoned his attention.

"Wake up," Clay said into Marisol's ear.

Marisol swatted sleepily at the source of noise. "Go 'way," she mumbled.

"No. Wake up," he insisted in a louder voice.

"Leave me alone." She burrowed her face deeper into the pillow. *"Caramba,* it's Sunday."

Clay gently lifted Marisol's upper body to a semi-sitting position. "I have to go to Jimmy. He's sick."

"Hunh?" she muttered, trying to focus on Clay's face. She'd spent a sleepless night, until finally at three o'clock in the morning she'd fallen asleep. But her slumber had been interrupted by recurring nightmares about the stalker. "What's wrong?"

"Jimmy is having a bout with asthma. I have to make sure he has the medicine he needs. I'll have my cell phone and beeper with me if you need to reach me."

"Tell Jimmy I hope he feels better," she said drowsily.

"Sure thing." Clay leveled a stern look at Marisol, pointing his finger at her. "Keep your little butt inside this apartment. Don't open the door to anyone either."

"Don't tell me what to do," she fumed.

"The last time I told you to stay put, you went for a little drive," Clay reminded her.

"I thought you weren't going to bring that up again!"

"If Jimmy wasn't sick, I'd stay here," Clay said, ignoring her protest. He walked to the door. "Don't let your guard down. I'll be back around noon."

In a huff, Marisol turned her back on him. "Just go," she mumbled into her pillow.

Eleven

The echo of heavy footsteps pounded in Marisol's ears. Her heart thudded in her constricting chest as her feet sank into the wet sand of the deserted beach. She forced her feet to carry her faster, but her leg muscles kept cramping painfully. The stalker was closing in on her. She stole a glance over her shoulder to gauge the distance between them. Less than ten yards away, she still couldn't make out his features in the dark. Fear and fatigue made her stumble in the sand.

Marisol let out a gulping cry as her foot stepped into a hole and she tripped, toppling face forward in agonizing slow motion. Her pursuer fell upon her, his hot body pressed against her lengthwise. She pushed backward with all her might, but his heavy weight forced her deeper in the murky sand. She tried to scream, but seawater and gravel rushed into her mouth. Large hands closed on her shoulders and turned her over. Marisol spewed the sand mixture into the man's face, but he wiped his face and laughed, grinding his hips against her with revolting intimacy.

Marisol still couldn't make out his features. She frantically blinked back the stinging salt water. Then

*she saw him. A primeval shriek ripped through her
lungs at the raw mass of flesh that made up his face.
Her throat raw from screaming, she took a deep,
shuddering breath. In the silence that ensued, she
heard the eerie sound of a distant bell, growing louder
and closer.*

Marisol bolted up from her prone position in bed,
her shaking body drenched in a cold sweat, her heart
thumping painfully inside her tight chest. Another
nightmare, this one more terrifying than the last! The
ringing bell in her dreams turned out to be the doorbell. She wondered why Clay wasn't answering the
door, then remembered that he'd left to attend to
Jimmy.

It was probably Marcos, come to make amends.
Marisol pushed herself out of her lethargy, slipped
into her sandals, and approached the door.

Clay returned to the apartment at noon. "Marisol,"
he called out. "I'm back." When no one answered, he
ran into the bedroom. Instead of finding Marisol, he
found Trini sitting on the bed, weeping.

"Where's Marisol?" he demanded.

"Ray was just here. He took her down the stairway," Trini wailed, her face swollen red as if she had
been slapped several times.

"Stay right where you are until the police get here,"
he ordered. "Otherwise I'll track you down."

Trini tearfully nodded. "I won't move. I promise,"
she blubbered. Eyes frantic, she clutched the sides of
her reddened face. "You have to believe me. Ray
forced me into this. I never thought he would go this
far to harm Marisol!"

"Ray has to be put away for good. He's sick. If you stay and cooperate with the police, we won't prosecute you." Clay really didn't care about Trini, and knew she'd never come near Marisol again. It was Ray he wanted.

"I'll stay."

Clay bolted out of the apartment, fearing that he wouldn't make it in time. He had to reach Marisol and save her. His blood ran ice-cold as he pondered Marisol's fate. She deserved far better. She had been his reason to get up each morning. He had never smiled so much in his life, nor loved so deeply. Why hadn't he told her this before? he wondered, tormented by a fresh wave of remorse.

Clay was tortured by the memory of the endearing words she had once said to him. *"I would love any child of ours. I have enough love in my heart for all types of children."*

Why, God? Why had he doubted Marisol's sincerity?

Gruesomely contorted, Ray Campbell's meaty face hovered inches away from Marisol's. "Shut up or I'll kill you." He kept his hand pressed against her mouth, stifling her protests.

Ray's fetid breath reeked of beer. When his spittle landed on her cheek, Marisol fought to control the bile rising in her throat. Her eyes felt like they were bulging and she moaned, trying to speak. But when she saw Ray reach for his gun, Marisol grew still and nodded in compliance. Marisol took a gulping breath and coughed when Ray removed his hot hand from her mouth.

"One peep out of you and you're dead," he warned.

He pressed the cold tip of his revolver against her rib cage and prodded her down the stairway. Taking an expeditious look around him, he pushed her along. In the hall, Marisol had been immobilized by the fear that Ray would shoot her if she screamed. Now she tried to reason with him.

"Ray, please don't do this; you'll go to jail!"

Ray ignored her plea and jabbed her forward. "I won't go to jail," he said with a brutal laugh. "I'm too smart for the police. I can fool anybody."

Marisol's stomach lurched when he shoved the gun harder against her rib cage. She stopped suddenly, her sandal's heel caught in the step. Her chest bursting with fear, she turned to Ray. "Why are you doing this? Don't you love Trini?"

"That slut? Now that she's pregnant with my baby, she's scrambling to please me," he jeered. "Trini is an expert seamstress. She made the satin handcuffs and the Barbie dress."

"I can't believe Trini would want to hurt me," she said.

Ray sneered. "Why not? I told her your business was ruining mine. After the last beating I gave her, Trini sweetly agreed to help me run you out of town." He weaved on the stairwell, snickering. "You always acted like such a stuck-up bitch. Prancing around in your high heels in skirts that showed off your naked legs and barely covered this sweet little ass. You flirted with everybody but me."

"That's not true. I always thought you were nice," she lied, frantically noting that his expression had turned uglier.

"You're lying. You never gave me the time of day!"

"I couldn't," she reasoned. "I knew Trini wanted to

date you, and even though I was attracted to you, Ray, I was already involved with Clay."

"Shut up! I know you're lying. Trini told me you convinced her to get the restraining order against me," he snarled drunkenly.

"That was only to protect her."

Ray's lower lip began to tremble pathetically. "Vanessa never loved me. She used to call me a pig and tell me no woman would ever marry me," he said, speaking in a singsong soprano voice.

"Who's Vanessa?" Marisol asked, trying to stall for time.

"The only girl I ever loved. But I can prove she was wrong. I can make you want me."

"What about Trini?" Marisol asked frantically. "I know she loves you."

"Trini doesn't count. I never wanted her." Ray startled Marisol by the abrupt change in his demeanor. His face turned pitifully childish, with tears streaming down his face. "You look like Vanessa, blond with slutty curves," he said.

He looked her up and down, half in lust and half in disgust.

"I'm gonna take you far away from here and break you like I did Trini. After I rough you up a few times, you'll be obedient, even if I have to drug you."

"No," Marisol said. "I'm not like Vanessa. I'm sure someday you'll find someone who will love you and want to marry you."

"Shut up, bitch! I don't want anybody else," he said, jabbing her back with the gun's nozzle. "Take off your sandals, they're slowing us down."

When Marisol obeyed his command, Ray spurred

her forward with another cruel thrust of his gun against her ribs. "You're not getting away from me this time."

Clay could hear voices from the stairway. He removed his shoes and clutched his Beretta as he opened the door. He began a mental chant: *stillness precedes motion, slowness precedes speed, softness precedes strength.* Those were the T'ai Chi basic foundations of motion, speed, and strength he had learned as a child and they had calmly carried him through many life-threatening situations.

Moving closer, Clay clearly heard Marisol cry, "Please, Ray! Let me go!"

He could just make out their shapes as he crept stealthily down the stairs leading to Ray and Marisol. Forcing himself to remain in control, Clay figured that Ray was holding a gun to Marisol as he coerced her down the stairwell. Clay realized he was shaking from fear for Marisol. He had difficulty forcing himself to concentrate solely on freeing Ray of the gun. Once again he attempted to cleanse his mind of distractions by chanting silently: *stillness precedes motion, slowness precedes speed, softness precedes strength.*

With phantom steps, he quietly crept up behind Ray. Clay performed a precise sweep-the-lotus kick aimed at his funny bone, successfully knocking the gun from his hand, down the length of the stairs.

Ray was instantly knocked against the railing. Clay chopped him on the back of the neck and knocked him unconscious. When Ray began to slide down the stairs, Clay yanked him by the back of his shirt and held him upright. He called out to Marisol. "Go to my apartment."

Paralyzed with fear, Marisol remained immobilized, watching as Ray regained consciousness and tried to ram his short, burly body against Clay. But Clay retaliated by slamming his gun against Ray's back and shoving him down the stairwell. Clay turned his head briefly and saw Marisol still standing there. "Go inside," he called out again. "I'll meet you there."

Downstairs, he handed Ray over to Alan. "Keep him in handcuffs until the police arrive."

His heart ready to burst with the frantic need to hold Marisol, Clay raced inside the building, rode up the elevator, and sprinted toward his apartment.

Marisol stood in the hallway. When she saw Clay, she ran toward him and fell into his arms. They stood locked in each other's embrace, neither moving for several moments.

Finally, Clay disengaged Marisol's tightly woven arms from around his neck and stood back to examine her for any trauma at Ray's hands. His heart clenched unbearably when he thought that he could have lost her forever. Noting that she was disheveled, but unharmed, he pulled her back into his arms and kissed her like a starved man. Releasing her briefly, he led her inside the condominium.

"Marisol, Marisol," he chanted, overcome by grief. "I almost lost you."

Marisol whimpered, "I know, Clay. Oh, God, I need you so much!"

Clay's chest constricted painfully with absolute love. Suddenly all the sweet words she needed to hear, the ones he had been reluctant and unsure how to say, came rushing out of his mouth with tormented sincerity.

"I love you, *mi amor,*" he whispered roughly. "I can't live without you," he said, not taking his eyes from Marisol's feverish gaze; then he devoured her mouth. He broke the kiss only to lift Marisol in a tight embrace. "I want to marry you. We'll have as many babies as you want," he promised hoarsely.

Locked together in a frenzied embrace, they rocked in unison.

"You're my own heart and soul. I love you more than life itself," he said with husky reverence.

Marisol clung to Clay and tears rolled down her cheeks as she rained kisses on his face. "I love you, too, *mi amor.* I never stopped loving you, even when I hated your deception."

Clay held her beloved face in his hands and gazed deeply into her passion-glazed eyes. "I could never live without you."

"Well . . . it's about time you saw the light, Blackthorne," she murmured, delighting Clay with her usual sass.

"You're damn right!" He chuckled and hugged her tightly.

"Did you mean it about wanting babies?" she asked, quirking a dainty eyebrow.

"How many do you want?"

"I'll settle for one," she said in a soft, enamored voice.

His shout of laughter rang through the room. "One? You might have to settle for two."

"What do you mean?"

"Twins run on both sides of my family."

"Dios mío. Mine, too!" Marisol hugged Clay exu-

berantly and reached up to lightly stroke the grooves beside his mouth. "Let's just hope they get your dimples."

"I'd rather they have your optimism," he countered.

They began planning their life together and Clay knew without a doubt that his life had been truly touched by sunshine.

Epilogue

Marisol closed her magazine and rose from the chair to see what all the commotion was about. She could hear the babies fussing from the upstairs nursery of their new home. She climbed the stairs, chuckling as she remembered Clay's shocked face when the doctor had announced she was expecting twins.

Just as the babies quieted, Marisol walked into the hallway. She stood in the doorway of the nursery, rooted to the spot observing the tender scene before her. Never in her wildest dreams would she have imagined her compelling husband to be serenading two tiny females at once.

Clay sat in Marisol's favorite rocking chair directly in front of the babies' cribs. A lock of jet-black hair spilled over his forehead as he bent over the guitar. His identical daughters cooed while he played for them. Just then, he glanced up and his dark eyes tenderly greeted her from across the room.

Continuing to strum the guitar, Clay winked at Marisol and sent her heart soaring.

COMING IN MAY 2001
FROM ENCANTO ROMANCE

__STARDUST
   by Diana Garcia   0-7860-1214-5 $3.99US/4.99CAN

Caught in a terrifying storm, Julia Huerta brings down her private plane on a remote landing strip that happens to belong to Tony Carrera. The reclusive country singer is now a single dad raising two kids on a ranch. His heart takes flight when the beautiful pilot unexpectedly lands in his arms. Neither of them is looking for love, but it might just be on the horizon . . .

__WAVES OF PASSION
   by Sylvia Mendoza   0-7860-1175-0 $3.99US/$4.99CAN

After years at sea, Lieutenant Commander Alex Rivera has realized something is missing from his life. It's time to settle down in his California hometown and experience the real world . . . and maybe even romance. And former Navy brat, Marissa Buenaventura, is the ideal candidate to initiate him into the joys of civilian life—like babies, barbecues, and all the other things a man can't live without . . .

USE THE COUPON ON THE NEXT PAGE TO ORDER

New Romances
From Encanto!

__**STARDUST**
by Diana Garcia
0-7860-1214-5
$3.99US/$4.99CAN

__**WAVES OF PASSIONS**
by Sylvia Mendoza
0-7860-1175-0
$3.99US/$4.99CAN

Call toll free **1-888-345-BOOK** to order by phone or use this coupon to order by mail. ALL BOOKS AVAILABLE MAY 1, 2001.

Name_____

Address _____

City_____ State _____ Zip _____

Please send me the books I have checked above.

I am enclosing $_____

Plus postage and handling* $_____

Sales tax (in NY and TN) $_____

Total amount enclosed $_____

*Add $2.50 for the first book and $.50 for each additional book.

Send check or money order (no cash or CODs) to: **Kensington Publishing Corp., Dept. C.O., 850 Third Avenue, New York, NY 10022**

Prices and numbers subject to change without notice. Valid only in the U.S.

All orders subject to availability. **NO ADVANCE ORDERS.**

Visit our website at **www.encantoromance.com**

All Latin	Cien por Ciento
All the Time	Todo el Tiempo

TOTALLATINO.COM

Subscribe to our INTERNRET service and enjoy a TOTALLATINO experience!

¡Subscribete a nuestro servicio de INTERNET y disfruta de una Experiencia Totalmente Latina¡

Latinlaffs, latinacorner, Sportsymás, TLKids, TLEntertainment, TLCyberNovelas and much more!

LOG ON NOW!!

¡CONECTATE AHORA!

For only $14.99 a month
Por sólo $14.99 al mes

THINK *YOU* CAN WRITE?
We are looking for new authors to add to our list.
If you want to try your hand at writing Latino romance novels,
WE'D LIKE TO HEAR FROM YOU!

Encanto Romances are contemporary romances with Hispanic
protagonists and authentically reflecting U.S. Hispanic culture.

WHAT TO SUBMIT

- A cover letter that summarizes previously published work or
  writing experience, if applicable.
- A 3-4 page synopsis covering the plot points, AND
  three consecutive sample chapters.
- A self-addressed stamped envelope with sufficient return
  postage, or indicate if you would like your materials recycled
  if it is not right for us.

Send materials to: Encanto, Kensington Publishing Corp.,
850 Third Avenue, New York, New York, 10022.
Tel: (212) 407-1500

Visit our website at
http://www.kensingtonbooks.com

¿CREE QUE PUEDE ESCRIBIR?

**Estamos buscando nuevos escritores. Si quiere
escribir novelas románticas para lectores hispanos,
¡NOS GUSTARÍA SABER DE USTED!**

Las novelas románticas de Encanto giran en torno a protagonistas
hispanos y reflejan con autenticidad la cultura de Estados Unidos.

QUÉ DEBE ENVIAR

- Una carta en la que describa lo que usted ha publicado
  anteriormente o su experiencia como escritor o escritora, si
  la tiene.
- Una sinopsis de tres o cuatro páginas en la que describa
  la trama y tres capítulos consecutivos.
- Un sobre con su dirección con suficiente franqueo.
  Indíquenos si podemos reciclar el manuscrito si no lo
  consideramos apropiado.

Envíe los materiales a: Encanto, Kensington Publishing Corp.,
850 Third Avenue, New York, New York 10022.
Teléfono: (212) 407-1500.

Visite nuestro sitio en la Web:
http://www.kensingtonbooks.com

ENCANTO QUESTIONNAIRE

We'd like to get to know you!
Please fill out this form and mail it to us.

1. How did you learn about *Encanto?*
   - ☐ Magazine/Newspaper Ad   ☐ TV ☐ Radio
   - ☐ Direct Mail   ☐ Friend/Browsing
2. Where did you buy your *Encanto* romance?
   - ☐ Spanish-language bookstore
   - ☐ English-language bookstore   ☐ Newstand/Bodega
   - ☐ Mail   ☐ Phone order   ☐ Website
   - ☐ Other_____
3. What language do you prefer reading?
   - ☐ English   ☐ Spanish   ☐ Both
4. How many years of school have you completed?
   - ☐ High School/GED or less   ☐ Some College
   - ☐ Graduated College   ☐ PostGraduate
5. Please cheek your household income range:
   - ☐ Under $15,000   ☐ $15,000-$24,999   ☐ $25,000-$34,999
   - ☐ $35,000-$49,999 ☐ $50,000-$74,999   ☐ $75,000+
6. Background:
   - ☐ Mexican   ☐ Caribbean_____
   - ☐ Central American_____ ☐ South American_____
   - ☐ Other_____
7. Name:_____ Age:_____
   Address:_____
   _____
   Comments: _____
   _____
   _____

Mail to:

Encanto, Kensington Publishing Corp., 850 Third Ave., NY, NY 10022